Me & Death

AN AFTERLIFE ADVENTURE

RICHARD SCRIMGER

TUNDRA BOOKS

Copyright © 2010 by Richard Scrimger

Published in Canada by Tundra Books,
75 Sherbourne Street, Toronto, Ontario M5A 2P9

Published in the United States by Tundra Books of Northern New York,
P.O. Box 1030, Plattsburgh, New York 12901

Library of Congress Control Number: 2008905360

Library and Archives Canada Cataloguing in Publication

Scrimger, Richard
        Me & death : an afterlife adventure / Richard Scrimger.

ISBN 978-0-88776-796-8

        I. Title.

        PS8587.C745M43 2010 jC813'.54 C2009-903678-6

We acknowledge the financial support of the Government of Canada
through the Book Publishing Industry Development Program (BPIDP)
and that of the Government of Ontario through the Ontario Media
Development Corporation's Ontario Book Initiative. We further
acknowledge the support of the Canada Council for the Arts and the
Ontario Arts Council for our publishing program. ONTARIO ARTS COUNCIL
                                                  CONSEIL DES ARTS DE L'ONTARIO

Design: Jennifer Lum
Typeset in Stone Informal
Printed and bound in Canada

1 2 3 4 5   15 14 13 12 11 10

Death in itself is nothing; but we fear
To be we know not what, we know not where.
                                        – John Dryden

A man came to a river and wished to cross, but
there was no bridge or ferry. He saw someone on
the far side and called out, "How do I get to the
other side of this river?" There was a pause and
then the reply: "What do you mean? You are on
the other side."

                                        – Old Joke

PART ONE

ME WHEN I WAS A PIECE OF CRAP

CHAPTER 1

I was walking up Roncesvalles, the big street in my neighborhood. Late June, late morning. Should have been at school but I wasn't because, well, because I didn't want to go. Hotter than spitting grease out – smells of tar and dust. Summer in the city. I moved slowly. Yawning. Enjoying the feel of the day around me. Other people being busy. Roncy has houses and apartment buildings on one side and stores on the other. I was on the store side, looking around. I stopped at the fruit place one block up from my house. K is the name on the sign. K FRUIT. The owner frowned at me. Little old Korean guy with his mouth turned down. I picked a plum from the baskets out front. I always waited until he was watching before I took stuff. I got a kick out of it because he looked so pissed, and there was nothing he could do. Arms like pencils sticking out of his short sleeves, dirty apron wrapped around and around his middle and tied in a bow. How could he hurt me? I was only in grade eight, but I was way bigger than him.

"Lousy plums today," I said.

"What you do?" He had an accent, made him hard to understand sometimes. He picked up a broom. Like that would scare me. "What you do, boy?" He stepped right up to me, but he was afraid. I could tell.

"Shut up." I had my mouth full. Maybe he couldn't understand me. Ha ha. Neither of us knew what the other was saying. What a yuck.

"Why you not in school?" he asked. "Go on, boy. Go." He made a sweeping motion with the broom.

"Why you talk funny?" I said.

I spat out the plum pit and walked away, one hand on my jeans to keep them up.

I was wearing my new shirt. I'd swiped it the day before from Goodwill, pulled it off the rack and put it on over my camo vest. Red shirt with a dragony pattern on it. Cashier was like, Did you have that shirt on coming in?

'Course, I said.

You sure? she said. 'Cause there's a price tag on it.

Sure as you're ugly, I said from the door.

The shirt freaked my big sister out when she saw it last night. That's your dead shirt! she screamed, jumping up, mouth a black-rimmed circle in her white face. You're dead, Jim! Dead! She ran past me up the stairs, skinny butt cheeks bouncing like tennis balls under her skirt.

What's with her? I asked Ma, dropping onto the couch. A commercial came on and she changed the channel. Belched a lungful of brown smoke.

Who knows? she said.

Cassie's four years older than me and, well, kind of strange, peering into empty corners, talking to shadows. One morning I went into her room because she was screaming. She was in bed, pointing at the ceiling, yelling at it to go away. And now my dead shirt, what was *that* about? My sister, what a freak-o.

I walked up Roncy past the donut shop and the pharmacy, and the Krakow Restaurant and the lawyer's office, eating my lousy plum and thinking back to last night. What a screwup it had been. What a mess.

The air conditioner above Jerry's door dripped onto the sidewalk, making a puddle. Jerry ran a Buy and Sell – saxophones and game systems over the counter, hot cars in the laneway garage with the double lock. I stepped over the puddle into the cool of the shop. Jerry, on the phone, nodded hello. I made my way to the pool table in the back room.

Sparks was doing push-ups on a patch of rug. Cap was leaning back in a broken chair, cell phone in hand, smoking. They were older than me – almost grown up. Cap was lean and dark-colored, and he wore a captain's hat. He was kind of slimy. He'd put his hand on your arm and you'd want him to take it off. Sparks was white, except for his tattoos – lightning bolts and barbed wire going up and down and around his arms. Lots of ink, because his arms were huge. Sparks was real stupid, but loyal – wherever Cap was, Sparks was nearby.

I said hi. Cap took a drag of his cigarette and flicked it at me. I caught it like a hot potato and stuck it in my mouth.

Sparks's body rose and fell like a piston. No effort, no change of pace. He could do push-ups forever.

"About last night," I said to Cap. "Did you find out what happened to Rafal? The cops –"

He must have signalled. Sparks caught my ankle in one hand and pulled hard. I fell, the cigarette spinning away. Sparks went back to his push-ups.

"No talking about last night." Cap never raised his voice.

"Yeah," said Sparks from the floor. "No talking."

"But it's important." I crawled to my feet. "Raf's my partner. I want to know what happened."

"That's your problem, Jim," said Cap. "You're too smart for your own good. You always want to know stuff. Isn't that right, Sparks?"

"Yeah," said Sparks. "Too smart."

Up, down, up, down. No strain in his voice at all.

"*I want to know* can get you in trouble, Jim. Sometimes it's better not to know. You understand that?"

"Yeah, but –"

I stopped myself before he had Sparks grab me again. "I mean, I understand," I said.

"*Good* for you, Jim. Very good."

His cell phone buzzed. He flipped it open, started pushing buttons. Sparks kept on pushing up. I left.

A black-and-orange cat sat on the curb, its mouth open in a yawn. I kicked it into the street. Stepped forward and down with the right foot, like a soccer goalie. Good thing Raf wasn't there – he has a thing about animals. Cat went flying over a heap of garbage bags right into the road, legs sprawled, then scrambled away like a hairy streak of lightning as an SUV slammed on the brakes.

I smiled, felt better. I hate cats. Hate 'em. Only now here was Lloyd with his face hanging out.

"What's *your* problem?" I said.

He was a couple of storefronts away from me. He took a step back, licked his lips.

"Don't like me kicking the cat, Lloyd? That it? How about I kick you instead?"

He turned and ran. I followed.

"Yeah, that's what I'll do!" I called. "I'll kick you like I kicked the stupid cat!"

Lloyd crossed Roncy. I noticed that even now, with me after him, he looked both ways before leaving the curb. What a ween. He had sniffles and freckles, and ate his lunch at home every day. He was probably on his way there right now. I'd been picking on him since kindergarten.

I leapt into the street. Someone called after me to watch out. I kept running. Lloyd's ginger-colored hair flapped up and down. I kept it in my sights. There was the warning voice again. "Watch out!" Something familiar about it.

I caught my trick ankle on the streetcar tracks and fell, hitting the back of my head. I'd had a problem with my ankle as long as I could remember. Mostly I could run and jump like everyone else, but now and then it folded over and I fell. No warning, I'd be walking along and suddenly I'd be on the ground. Happened once in the middle of a game of HORSE, cost me my shot. I wanted to do it over, but Raf said rules are rules.

This was another bad time for my ankle to go. The world flickered off and on like a faulty connection.

On: I was lying in the middle of Roncesvalles. Smell of pavement and diesel exhaust, with a hint of baking from the donut shops. An ear-shattering shriek of brakes and a long skid.

Off.

On: A beat-up blue Pontiac – I recognized the grille – was almost on top of me. The driver stared down at me with eyes as big as Ferris wheels.

Off.

On: Tadeusz standing next to me. Tadeusz! Of all people. He bent over to peer at me, closely.

CHAPTER 2

"Hi, Jim."

I stood up, shook myself. Said hi.

"You recognize me?"

"Yeah. I heard your voice, telling me to watch out," I said.

We stepped away from the accident. Cars were stopped all around us. Horns blowing, people calling out. The driver of the blue Pontiac was leaning on her front fender.

"Are you frightened of me, Jim?"

"We-ell . . ."

Tadeusz was a legend on Roncy. Started out stealing radios from parked cars, and by the time he graduated high school he owned a half-dozen houses. Cap was his second in command. Tadeusz wore tailored suits, and he ripped up parking tickets and boasted that he could eat an entire roast chicken at a sitting. Once, he gave me fifty bucks to go into the donut shop, buy a coffee and cruller, and bring them out to his double-parked Jaguar because he didn't want to turn off the song on the radio. That was a couple of years ago. There was a big write-up in the newspapers when he was shot dead at the age of twenty-two. They never found out who did it.

"You *are* a ghost, aren't you?" I said.

The only other explanation was that this was a dream. And it didn't seem like a dream. Too vivid. The crowd around us was growing. People were screaming and calling out. I recognized a lot of neighborhood faces. Mrs. Solarski from the pharmacy had her hand clamped over her mouth. The driver of the Pontiac was sobbing. In the distance I could see the flashing light on the top of a cop car.

"I'm what they call a Mourner. Kind of a ghost."

"So I guess I'm a little scared," I said.

"Good!"

"Good?" I said. "What's good about it?"

"I want you scared, Jim. You're a piece of crap, and I want to frighten you."

CHAPTER 3

He took me by the arm and led me away from the crowd. We stood on the sidewalk by the public library, in the shade of a maple tree.

"Look at me," he said.

I rubbed my arm. It was cold from where he touched it.

Tadeusz held his hands away from his body and turned around like a fashion model.

"How do I look?" he said.

I shrugged. I didn't want to upset him.

"You remember what I used to be, Jim? I was the king of Roncesvalles, wasn't I? I was like the Godfather. I could walk into the Krakow Restaurant and get the table at the window any time I wanted. There was a hostess who would save it for me. Jolanda. She's still there. I . . ." A spasm crossed his face and he looked away. "Point is, Jim, I'm not the king now. Do I look like a king?"

I shook my head. His body was sunk in on itself, like a rotten piece of fruit. His trademark suit flapped and bagged around his shrunken paunch. Of course the blood and bullet holes didn't help.

And he was ghostly in color. Suit, shirt, shoes, hair, eyes, skin – all as gray as fog.

"You look pretty bad," I said.

"Do you know what a ghost is, Jim? A ghost is a guy who was a piece of crap when he was alive."

"But you weren't!" I said. "You were the bomb. I thought you were the coolest!"

"I lied, I stole, I hurt people. I let them down. I was a bad guy, Jim."

I struggled with this. "Yeah, but you were a *good* bad guy," I said.

He smiled sadly. "I like you, Jim," he said. "You remind me of me, when I was young."

"Thanks."

"Shut up. Pay attention to what I say. You do not want to be a ghost. Ghosts are in pain. That's why we're hanging around. Do you want to be like me when you die, Jim? Staying at the Jordan Arms, and wandering up and down Roncesvalles for years and years – maybe forever? And sad. That's what Mourners are – sad ghosts. I'm so sad I'd kill myself if I wasn't already dead."

He coughed – a long, racking one.

"Sorry, Jim. It's like there's something stuck inside me and I can't get it out."

Truly he was a changed guy – the Tadeusz I remembered did not apologize for anything.

Traffic on Roncy was stopped. Cars idled in the heat of a summer noontime. The nearest one was a Civic with blacked-out windows. It vibrated from the bass beats inside.

I thought about being Tadeusz like he used to be. I imagined myself driving a cool car, getting out of it to beat people up, driving away again. I'd sleep late, play pool, start fires. Raf and I could hang out together in our own place, so he wouldn't have to live with his dad and I wouldn't have to live with Cassie. Cap and Sparks would ask my permission to do things.

It's good to be the king. But Tadeusz wasn't a king now, sniveling and coughing up his lungs. It would *not* be great to end up like him.

"You have been given a gift," he told me. "A great chance. Come with me."

Tadeusz led me back to the front of the Pontiac. No one noticed us. One guy turned around and looked right through us.

"Here you are, Jim."

A boy's body lay on the ground with his legs under the front of the car and his eyes closed. I knew his face from the mirror in the bathroom at home. The body was mine.

"You're lucky," said Tadeusz.

"Because I'm going to die?"

"Because you're not."

Lying-down-me was breathing, I noticed. But I was clearly unconscious. The Pontiac driver was on her knees beside me, weeping. A whole bunch of old people were shaking their heads and talking about how awful the traffic was these days.

Old people drive you crazy.

"You sure I'm going to make it?" I said to Tadeusz.

He nodded. "You're in a coma."

Lying-down-me had a rip in his shirt – like I did. His cheek was bloody. And (reaching up and having my hand come away red) so was mine. Huh. I wiped it on my pants.

"That's my great chance? A coma?"

"You're going to have a near-death experience. In fact, you're having it right now."

I noticed a woman floating in midair. She wore a hospital gown, kind of billowy, and a cap on her head. She looked sad and anxious – like someone's mom. She hovered about telephone pole height, peering down at the scene of the accident.

Tadeusz noticed her too. He waved.

"That's Denise up there. She's going to take you to the Jordan Arms for the day. Pay attention to her, Jim, and to everything else that happens to you there."

"Uh-huh. What is this Jordan Arms? Sounds like a bar."

I was still staring up. You don't see flying women every day.

Tadeusz grabbed my shoulder. "I'm serious, Jim. You'll get a chance to watch your past there. You'll see the people you've let down and hurt. Remember those people when you wake up in the hospital. Treat them better. Change! Don't be such a piece of crap. Or you'll end up like me."

It was like his hand was dry ice. My shoulder burned, it was so cold.

"You are standing in wet cement, Jim. All the fear and anger, all the sadness in your life ties you down. When you die the cement sets, and you're trapped. Today is your chance. Learn from the past, so you can climb out while the cement is still wet."

He turned to go. I rubbed my shoulder, trying to warm it up.

"Let me get this straight," I said. "Sounds like what you're saying is that you want me to be *nice* to people. Is that it? Is that the great secret?"

He looked back. "I wish I had known, before I died. I wish I had had your chance, Jim."

"Yes, yes, but . . . *nice*?" It sounded so lame. "Nice?" I raised my voice. "Saying please and thank you? Helping old ladies? Using my napkin?"

He was gone, skimming through the crowd with his feet barely touching the pavement. I had to laugh. Tadeusz used to collect his rents with a baseball bat. He'd beat people up for exercise. One time Raf saw him push a kid through a storm door. A little kid – smaller than me, Raf said. She ended up on her back on the sidewalk, covered in bits of window glass. And now this super-tough guy was begging me to be nice. It was just, well – funny. I laughed and laughed.

CHAPTER 4

Denise touched down beside me with a gentle bump.

"You're Jim." Gloomily.

"Yeah."

She peered at lying-down-me, checking his face against mine. Nodded to herself, like I was a parcel she was signing for.

"Yeah, that's you. I'm Denise."

"I know."

She frowned.

"*You know,*" she said heavily. "Yes, you do. You know a lot for a crappy little kid. Do you know how you became a piece of crap?"

"Hey!" I said.

"Well, let's find out." She took my hand, and we floated away like balloons.

Maybe *floated* is the wrong word. We moved upward slowly, with pauses, like a roller coaster going chunk, chunk, chunk up that first hill. It was a little queasy-making. I've never liked rides much.

Her hand was as cold as Tadeusz's. I tried to pull away, but I couldn't. She was stronger than me. I gave up. We were getting too high to jump anyway.

———

They weren't moving my body, I noticed. Someone had backed the Pontiac off me and covered me with a blanket, though.

"You had a bad accident, Jim," said Denise. "But you're not dying."

"Yeah. Tadeusz explained. You're going to take me to the Jordan Arms. I'm supposed to pay attention to you because I'm stuck in concrete."

"What?"

"Forget it. Something he said."

We were at rooftop level now and still rising. An ambulance was making its way slowly up Roncy. Lloyd stood on the curb with his mouth open. Little ween. Wait 'til I got hold of him. I was in a coma now, but I'd be back, and then he'd get his.

My pants started to slip. I grabbed them with my free hand.

Higher than the apartment buildings, and still rising. Cars looked like dots. We floated side by side, not looking at each other, like you do in an elevator with a stranger, both of you watching the numbers change in silence.

"You sure this isn't a dream?" I said. "I'm flying."

"Do you often fly in dreams, Jim?"

"Sure. Don't you?" I laughed at myself. What a dummy. "'Course you fly in dreams. You're in this one of mine."

"This isn't a dream," she said with a sigh. "I only wish it were."

What a Gloomy Gladys.

I wondered how she died. She wasn't that old. No wrinkles. Her hair was gray, but that was because she was a ghost – it'd be dark if she were alive. Her skin was midway between light and dark. Her gray hand was cleaner than mine. Like a teacher's hand. Polish on the nails.

We slowed to a halt, hovering like bugs or helicopters. I could feel her disapproving of me. I'm used to that – most people disapprove of me. Teachers, store owners, streetcar drivers. My sister. I'm used to it, but I don't like it. I opened my mouth to tell her to shut up when I noticed a jet flying right at us.

From the ground, jets look like they're taking their time, but up close they really move. This one had been a speck on the horizon a few seconds ago, and now it filled the sky. As it roared beneath us, I saw into the cockpit. Two guys in shirtsleeves, one of them fiddling with a dial, the other one drinking coffee. They didn't see us, but we must have made some kind of turbulence because the plane shuddered as it went by and the guy spilled his coffee. I laughed. The plane sped away, vanishing as quickly as it had appeared.

Denise made a fist with her free hand and began swinging it in front of her. Blind, flailing punches.

"What are you doing?"

She didn't answer my question. Below us, the wind drove one puffy white cloud into another one. They looked like two billiard balls. When they hit, I half expected the target cloud to move off at a ninety-degree angle, like a billiard ball would. Didn't happen. They came together to make one rounded cloud with a point at the top, like a big white teardrop. The horizon bent away into the distance.

Denise was still punching the air. "Come on. I know it's around here somewhere," she said, a hint of exasperation in her voice.

"What is?"

Her left fist made a hollow knocking sound.

"This." She felt around and grabbed a piece of sky. I didn't know how – it was all blue to me. But she found a piece to grab on to and pulled. There was a creaking sound, and a door-sized section of blue opened in front of us.

"Welcome to the Jordan Arms," she said gloomily.

She pulled me through the door in the sky and shut it behind us.

CHAPTER 5

What a dump. Reminded me of the Edgewater Hotel, down at the foot of Roncy. My ma used to fall asleep in the bar there, and I'd have to walk her home. This place was even worse than the Edge, though – dimmer, shabbier, dustier, staler. And completely colorless. From cobwebbed ceiling to sticky floor, the Jordan Arms and everyone in it were shades of black and white and gray. I felt like I was in an old movie.

A gray couple sitting on a rickety couch with their hands in their laps stared at me. So did the gray guy picking his teeth, leaning against a pillar.

I took a deep breath and let it out. There's a moment when you accept the logic of your dream and it ceases to be scary. *This is your world, for now. Here are your friends, and enemies. This is your job.* So Jordan Arms was like my life, only uglier.

Fair enough.

I followed Denise to the front desk with my right hand clamped under my armpit to warm it up. The granny behind the desk looked familiar. Maybe because she wore a dark kerchief. I saw a lot of women like her on Roncy. They were usually shaking a cane at me because I was making a noise or a mess. Raf called them all *baba* – his word for granny.

Her name tag read, *Orlanda*.

"This is Jim, from Garden Avenue," said Denise. "He's here for the day. He'll be going back."

"I know who he is." Orlanda pulled her sweater around her bony shoulders and split her face in a frown of disapproval. Dentures like tombstones.

She made me sign the register and handed me a plastic day pass.

"Not that you need it," she said.

I knew what she meant. The hotel may have been black and white, but I was in color – I guess because I wasn't dead yet. In my dragon shirt and blue jeans, I stood out like a searchlight.

I put the pass in my pocket.

The old couple from the couch tottered over. He didn't want to come, but she pulled him along. She had a nose like a parrot's beak. Pretty Polly, only she wasn't pretty at all. She pointed at my shirt.

"Red," she said miserably. Like it was the saddest thing in the world that my shirt was red.

"Yeah."

She smelled like old people – wool and liniment and that gasoline reek that seems to come from the flaps and folds of dead skin.

Her man didn't have a beard exactly but a few whiskers curled over the bottom half of his chin, hiding its retreat.

He wasn't sad, like Polly. He was scared. I knew the look. Reminded me of Lloyd. He was sweating with fear, this guy. Made me mad.

"What's the matter with *you*?" I snapped at him.

He whimpered, turned away.

I stepped toward him. Ugly old badger, I'd punch him in the throat.

Denise leapt between us.

"No," she said.

"What the –"

She pushed me backward, both hands on my chest like what's-her-name from *Seinfeld*. Man, she had cold hands! "Don't be such a jerk, Jim," she said. "What in heaven's name do you want to fight a Grave Walker for? What's the point?"

"He needs a lesson! He . . ." I stopped. "Grave Walker? What do you mean?"

"He's a Grave Walker. Like I'm a Mourner. No point in fighting me either. You can't beat a ghost, Jim."

"Right! He's a ghost. You're not real. You're a ghost, aren't you?" I called after the old man. But he and Polly were moving away.

"I showed him," I said.

"You've got a lot of learning to do," said Denise sadly.

"You ever thought of wearing gloves?"

We went up the wide staircase to the second floor. A threadbare carpet stretched into the distance. Through an archway I saw an ice maker, and a vending machine, and the guy who had been picking his teeth downstairs. He gaped at me, wide-eyed, toothpick hanging from his lower lip, a package of jelly beans in his hand.

I wondered what gray jelly beans would taste like.

Next door down said, GAMES. We went in. The room was teeny – no bigger than my bedroom at home. Inside was a card table and chairs, and a TV with a treadmill in front of it.

Looked like we were the only ones who had been here in a while. Dust coated everything like icing.

Denise told me to get on the treadmill.

"No," I said.

She didn't say anything.

"Why should I?" I said. "I don't want to run on a stupid treadmill. I want to watch TV."

"You can watch TV while you are on the treadmill," she said.

I got the remote from on top of the TV, dragged over a chair from the card table, and sat down. "No," I said firmly.

I wondered what she'd do now. I wasn't fighting her, exactly. I was just being decisive. Back home, Ma would walk away shaking her head when I acted like this. I didn't try it often with Cassie because she was so unpredictable. (One time she asked me to save her some Frosted Flakes, but I poured them all into my bowl anyway. She got right up from the table, went to the store, bought another box of cereal, and emptied the whole thing onto my bed, along with the rest of the bag of milk.)

Denise sighed and put her hands on her hips. "Why do you continue behaving like a piece of crap, Jim?"

"Hey!"

"You must be one of the very stupidest people I have ever met. This experience – this visit to the Jordan Arms –

is a one-in-a-million chance, Jim. Don't throw it away. Pay attention right here, right now. You will see the chains that tie you to Earth while you still have time to free yourself from them. You're ripping up a winning lottery ticket. That's how stupid you are. Didn't Tadeusz explain things to you? He's worried about you – he says you behave almost as badly as he did at your age."

"You're the stupid one," I said. "You're the ghost. Not me."

Denise put her hands up to her head. I had a teacher who did that just before he sent me to the principal's office.

"I was stupid, all right," she said. "But I'm not now. I would give anything – anything except the life of my child – to have had your chance today, Jim. To see where I was going wrong while I could still change it. This is a preview of your existence after your die. Do you wish to spend forever here? Forever?"

The gray, the dust, the unbroken circle of quiet pain.

"'Course not," I said. "Who'd want to live in this dump? But I don't have to. That's the whole point. I'm here visiting, right? I'm not going to die. I'll wake up in a hospital. Oh, and by the way – Tadeusz used to be cool, but now that he'd dead he's acting real lame."

I pointed the remote at the TV and pushed the power button. The TV came on – in color, which was a relief – but there was something wrong with it. The picture was frozen. I pressed the other buttons. The scene didn't change. Looked like part of an old movie, two little kids in an upstairs hall. Grainy film. But –

"Hey!"

I stood up, went closer. "Hey, I know where that is."

Get this: the movie was of my place. I recognized the upstairs hall. Our wallpaper was cleaner in the movie, and the railing was fixed, but it was home. The girl looked familiar too. The baby looked like any baby. Grubbier than usual, maybe. Shirt, diaper, feet. The girl wore a striped skirt and sandals, looked like she was in kindergarten. She glared at the baby.

"That's Cassie!" I pointed at the screen. "Isn't it? And that's the upstairs at our house. There's the bathroom at the end, with no door handle. What a yuck. I'm right, aren't I? That's my sister."

"That's her," said Denise. "Twelve years ago."

"She was a freaky-looking little kid, wasn't she? Who's the baby?"

Denise's voice came in a whisper. "That's you."

Oh.

CHAPTER 6

There aren't any family pictures in our house. I'd never seen myself as a baby – still haven't, come to think of it, except this once. I stared at the screen, couldn't get over it. Me. And do you know what I was doing? Smiling. Me. Smiling like a bastard because I could walk. What a stupid goof. Looking at myself, I felt a lump in my chest, like when you have to burp. I tried working the remote again. None of the buttons did anything. Piece of junk.

"Want to watch the show?" asked Denise from behind me.

I nodded.

"Maybe the TV will work if you get on the treadmill," she said.

I shot her a look. Her face was blank.

"Yeah, maybe."

I got on, pressed a button, and found myself walking to keep from falling backward. The movie started slow and uneven. There were pauses. It didn't look natural at all. It was like I was reading the film, not watching it.

INT. HALLWAY – DAY.
JIM (2) totters toward his sister, CASSIE (6). He beams at her, toothless. She glares back at him.

JIM

Gah! Gah!

CASSIE

Do you see the ball, Jim?

JIM

Gah.

I walked faster, and faster, and finally broke into a run, swinging my arms to keep my balance. The movie picked up too, until it was playing at regular speed.

"How is this happening?" I nodded at the screen. "Where's the camera?"

"There is no camera," said Denise. "This is your past. You're lying in the middle of Roncesvalles Avenue right now, with a subdural hematoma."

Oh, yeah.

I felt the baby's feelings as my own. When he staggered forward on the screen, I felt proud of myself. When he fell, I was surprised too. I ran harder, focusing on the screen, as if my effort could help the poor baby, struggling to pick himself up.

"Good!" Denise's voice came from a long way off.

The TV picture got bigger, clearer, closer. It filled my vision. For a second, it was like I was inside the set, looking back at the dusty games room. Then I found myself in a full-color world – my hall at home. I wasn't on the treadmill anymore. I floated in the air in front of the bathroom door, staring down at the baby I used to be.

I was inside the TV picture, a witness to my own past. Weird? Oh, yeah. And kind of awful. You ever wake up in the middle of the night and you're not sure who you are? It was like that, only worse. I was two people here. And still panting from my exertion on the treadmill.

"Well done, Jim." Denise floated next to me. She was still in her hospital gown, still black and white and gray.

"Shut . . . up." That felt a little better.

If it weren't for recognizing the hallway and my sister, I'd swear that kid wasn't me. I couldn't remember ever hugging Cassie, but here he was with his hands around her waist and a big smile. When she dropped a red-and-yellow plastic ball, he hurried to get it for her. Who was this guy?

Cassie took the ball and pushed him away so that he fell back on his diaper. Still smiling. She got this cunning look on her face.

Jim, she whispered. *Oh, Jim . . .*

I felt sick. I knew that look.

The baby smiled when he heard his name. *Gah gah,* he said.

Cassie held the ball up so that the baby could see it and tossed it gently over the railing. Steep wooden stairs on the other side. The ball bounced a couple of times on its way down to the front hall.

Jim, she said, the way you talk to a dog. *Go get the ball, Jim.*

He grinned, slapping his dirty bare feet on the wooden floor of the hall as he staggered along. He stopped at the top of the staircase.

"No, Jim!" I shouted. "No!"

"He can't hear you."

Denise put her hand on my arm. Sympathetic. I shook it off.

Twelve years ago. That's why there wasn't any mold on the wallpaper. The hall railing didn't have a piece missing because it hadn't been broken yet.

Cassie pointed down the stairs. *Get the ball, Jim. Go on.*

"Ma! Where are you?" I shouted.

"She's out. You know that."

I sighed.

"You can't do anything," said Denise. "You can't change what's happened."

So we watched. Jim couldn't decide whether to walk down the stairs or go backward on his hands and knees. Cassie decided for him, giving him a hard two-handed push. He landed on the fourth or fifth step, bounced once, and rolled to the bottom of the stairs. Watching, I felt a kind of shadow of what he was feeling. When he landed sideways on the step, my left side hurt. When his foot got caught briefly in the banister, my trick ankle hurt. When he banged into the wall, my head hurt.

Baby Jim lay in a heap on the dusty linoleum. Cassie ran downstairs with a smile like broken glass. She bent low over him.

Now you don't work, Jim! she said. *You don't work, and Mommy will throw you out, like the video when it didn't work. Then there will only be me.*

She did a dance, swinging her rake-handle body back and forth. Her long dark hair swished around her head. *Only me!* She sang. *Only me.*

I tugged on Denise's bare arm. "Why does Cassie hate Jim so much?"

She shook her head.

The lump was in my chest again, bigger than ever. "He – I – the baby liked her. He gave her hugs, and she . . ."

Denise looked even sadder than usual. "Yes, I know."

Cassie kept dancing. It was hard to watch.

"Why don't I remember this?" I said. "Am I too young?"

Denise and I floated downward. Dust motes jumped and swirled below us, golden in the late-afternoon light.

"You do remember, Jim," she said. "That's why we're here. If you didn't remember it, it couldn't haunt you."

She pointed to the baby, crying feebly. "See, you're awake."

I heard a bumping sound at the front door. A key fumbling in the lock. Cassie heard it too. She broke off her dance and ran upstairs. When she reached me and Denise, she stopped for a moment. We blocked her path, floating side by side, a little above floor level. Her bright blue eyes were full of fear.

"She can't see us," said Denise.

It seemed like she was aware of us, though. She raced past me with her head down.

Ma half stumbled through the door, looking way younger than she does now. Scary to think what twelve years can do.

Sorry I'm late! she called. *I only stepped out for a moment, but this man kept buying me drinks.*

The closer she came, the smaller and farther away she got. Baby Jim was falling asleep. The scene got smaller and dimmer, and then I was back on the treadmill in the games room of the Jordan Arms, staring at a blank TV screen, and panting like I'd just run a marathon.

CHAPTER 7

Waking from a nightmare is a relief. But this was like waking from one dream into another. I was still a long way from my bed at home. My legs shook. I got off the treadmill like an old man climbing out of a roller coaster. I made it to a chair and sat down. I couldn't get the images out of my head: the baby with the toothless smile, and the sister who hated him, and the mother who wasn't there.

"How do you feel, Jim?" asked Denise.

"I don't know."

"You must feel wretched. I know I would. There was so much sadness in that brief scene. So much that you lost."

"Are you talking about my ankle?" I said.

"No."

"'Cause I've had a bad ankle as long as I can remember. I didn't know I twisted it falling down those stairs. My ankle turned over when I was crossing Roncy just now. That's why I fell."

She sighed deeply.

"You lost more than your ankle on the stairs, Jim."

I thought back to what Tadeusz had told me. *You'll see people you need to treat better*, he said. Who was he talking about? Cassie? Ma? I didn't understand. I didn't understand at all.

Denise suggested we go across the hall and get a drink. I said sure. I didn't want to look at any more TV just now.

The vending machines crouched side by side like football linemen. I wanted a Coke and a chocolate bar, but the only drink in the soft-drink machine was ginger ale, and the candy machine was out of everything except Junior Mints.

Denise got a coffee for herself and showed me how to swipe my day pass to get my snack.

She took a sip and sighed. "Coffee's always too cold here," she said.

I wondered why a ghost would want coffee at all, whatever the temperature.

One of the fluorescent lights was off – it flickered and buzzed overhead. Irritating. We went back into the hall. I ate a mint. It was chocolate-coated, and I'd eat dog food if it was chocolate-coated – but it tasted pretty bad.

Man, this hotel sucked!

"How long have you been here?" I asked.

"Fourteen years."

As long as I'd been alive.

There was a battered couch by the wall. We sat down on it, releasing plumes of dust into the air. Denise talked about how she died, after giving birth to her first child. Pretty dramatic story. Last-minute cab to the hospital. Fainting. Mess and doctors everywhere. Shouting husband. Pain. More pain. A tiny, coughing baby. Weakness. Cold. And then oceans of blood.

Yeck.

"I held my son as I died," she said. "It was so sad. I was filled with such regret at all the things I wouldn't see."

She sniffed a little. I took a sip of ginger ale.

"What kind of things?" I said.

"Everything! I'd miss him teething and crying and going off to kindergarten, and picking me a bouquet of dandelions, and learning how to tell time. I'd miss him scraping his knee and falling in love, and going off to soccer practice, and graduating. All sorts of things."

She sighed.

"You sure your baby was a boy?" I asked.

She glared at me. "What do you mean?"

"Nothing. Just a joke."

"I don't joke," she said.

I took a sip of ginger ale.

"I've never spoken to him," she said. "Never told him I love him. Do you think he knows, Jim? Does he realize that his mother loves him more than anything else in the world?"

She had been pretty tough down on the street, calling me a piece of crap. Now fat tears rolled down her face like trucks down a rainy highway.

"I don't know," I said.

I've never seen my dad. Never spoken to him. I've asked Ma about him a few times, and she says different things. Sometimes she's poetic, sometimes forgetful. Once, she said he was like a sunset – red and fiery and headed for the horizon. Another time she told me he got real sick after I was born and had to go away. I asked her what was the matter with him. With who? she said. Dad, I said. What about him? she said. I want to know what was wrong with him, I said. You want a list? she said. I told her it was okay, and that I was going to bed.

Does he love me? I'm going to say: *No.*

Denise was on her feet. "I can't take it anymore. It's been hours. I've got to see him," she wailed. "I've got to see my boy right now."

She dropped her empty Styrofoam cup and hurried down the hall. I followed.

"What happens to me?" I asked. We were at the top of the wide staircase leading down to the lobby.

"Don't move, Jim. A Grave Walker will come for you," she said.

"A what?"

But she didn't answer.

She'd called that old guy in the lobby a Grave Walker. The guy I wanted to beat up. Was he coming for me? I hoped not.

The front door of the hotel was open, and a vivid blue rectangle of sky dominated the gray of the lobby. Out there, and a long way down, was my body. It was a weird moment. What am I saying – the whole day was weird. But that moment at the top of the stairs, looking at the world outside – that was among the weirdest.

Denise raced down the stairs and across the lobby, drawn back to Earth by her ties to a boy the same age as me.

CHAPTER 8

Before Denise reached the door, two people entered through it into the hotel. First was a bearded guy. I didn't notice much else about him. The girl beside him, though, grabbed my attention with both hands.

I took a step down and sat on the top step to watch her. She was older than me. But not much older. Fifteen, maybe sixteen. Her hair was damp, worn shoulder length and pushed carelessly off her long angular face. She frowned now, worrying away at her wide lower lip. At this distance I couldn't make out much about her eyes, but I imagined them to be deep and dark. She wore a dressing gown open over her hospital gown. She looked like an elf queen – maybe what's-her-name from *The Lord of the Rings* only without the goofy ears.

I'd seen her before. She lived in my neighborhood. But I'd never noticed her. Maybe dying brought out her natural whatever it is. Or mine. She looked hot, I tell you.

She got her day pass from Orlanda at the front desk and walked across the lobby, head high. I stood. She was near the foot of my staircase now. She looked up, saw me, and stopped. So did the awful music playing in the background. I'd been trying to ignore it ever since I arrived at the hotel – headache-making stuff you'd expect to hear over the phone while you were on hold. Anyway, it vanished now, leaving only a breathing silence, and me, and the girl.

I took a step and almost lost my balance. Ironic, after that childhood scene I had just witnessed. I grabbed the banister to steady myself. Kept walking. The girl smiled and pushed her hair back. Her dressing gown had blue teddy bears on it.

We met at the bottom of the stairs. I stopped. I was drawn to her like a needle to a magnet . . . but I didn't know what to say.

She spoke.

"You're in color too!" Her voice was husky.

"Uh, yeah." I took a breath. Seemed like I'd been holding that last one in for a while. I noticed the awful music again.

"You know what that means?"

"Yeah. I'm here visiting. You and me, we're not going to die."

"Well, not today."

We laughed together. Her breath smelled spicy. I was close enough to see her eyes now. Dark like her hair.

The bearded guy put a hand on her arm. "We have to go, Marcie," he said sadly. "It's time for your vision of sorrow."

"Give me a second," she said, without turning her head.

I couldn't take my eyes off her. Yeah, she was hot, but she was also someone else going through what I was going through. It was like she was proof that what was happening to me was real. Not a dream.

"Marcie, eh?" I said. "I'm Jim. From the neighborhood. You know." I pointed at the floor. "Down there."

"Yeah, I've seen you on Roncy."

She hesitated and then held out her hand. I took it. It was soft and warm. I can't tell you the last time I shook a girl's hand. Never, I think. I didn't know the right time to let go. She was the one who finally pulled away. An awkward moment, and yet at the same time not.

"So you're sick, huh?" I said, gesturing at her gown.

"Oh. Yeah. Yeah, I'm in the hospital. Some kind of high fever. I got up to go the bathroom and passed out. You?"

"Car ran me down," I said.

"Bummer."

We laughed again. There was a kind of click inside me. I don't know what else to call it. It seemed to go all down my back. She felt it too, like she and I were following the same thought along the same set of nerve endings. How do I know she felt it? Good question.

"I thought I was dreaming," she said. "I mean . . . floating up to the sky and finding a hotel. That sounds ridiculous. But if it could happen to you too, then maybe I'm not dreaming. Know what I mean?"

"Oh yeah."

The bearded guy grabbed Marcie's arm. "Time to go," he said. He had a nasal voice. I didn't like him. She protested, but he was stronger. He pulled her upstairs. The soles of her bare feet were dirty, I noticed. After a few steps she stopped struggling and went along with him. Denise had been stronger than me too.

A little kid stood about spitting distance away from me, staring at me quite openly, the way they do.

"What's your problem?" I said.

He didn't answer. His thumb was in his mouth with his first finger curled around the top of his nose. I figured he was interested in me because of the color thing. I was alive and he wasn't.

"Beat it!" I said.

He shivered but didn't beat it. Just kept sucking his thumb. His gray curly hair hung wet and limp in a modified Afro. He wore camper-style shorts and knee socks. He was scared. And there was something . . . *off* about him too. Why didn't he run away?

The lobby was empty. Just me and the dust and the carpeting and this creepy kid. I went right up to him, thinking to scare him off. He took his thumb out of his mouth and made a mewing sound, like a cat.

Stopped me dead.

I hate cats. This little kid sounding just like one – out of no place like that – scared the crap out of me. I froze. I thought of the cat I had kicked onto the street. Which made me think of my friend Raf, who liked cats. Which made me think of the last time I'd seen Raf, under the dash of the big white Lincoln. What a screwup!

I couldn't move, not even when the kid reached up to take my hand in his. I didn't want to touch his spit-sticky fingers, but I had no choice.

"I'm Wolfgang," he said. "It's time for your second vision, Jim."

He dragged me past the staircase to the elevator.

CHAPTER 9

T here was room for both of us in the elevator – barely.
It was one of those slooooow ones. Lots of creaking
and whining. Took us a long minute to get to the
third floor. I kept thinking we were going to get stuck.

When Wolfgang let go of my hand, I wiped it dry.

His hand wasn't the only wet thing about him. His
face ran with sweat, and the collar of his T-shirt was
darker than the rest of it. When he shifted his weight, I
swear I heard squishing sounds from his shoes.

He trembled a lot. As the elevator hitched and
groaned its way up, I'd look down at him, and he'd have
his thumb in his mouth and his eyes closed. And he'd be
shaking. Tadeusz had said that ghosts were tied to Earth.
That's why they were staying at this pathetic hotel. Pretty
clear that Denise was here because of her son. I wondered
what tied Wolfgang. Did he feel sad because he never got
to grow up? That didn't sound right. When I was his age
I didn't regret anything. What have you done wrong by
the time you're six?

I asked him if he was a Mourner. He shook his head.

"Grave Walker," he said without taking his thumb
out of his mouth. Sweat dripped from the ends of his hair.

The elevator stopped, finally, and we got out. The
third-floor hall had spiderwebs and peeling wallpaper.
Bare lightbulbs hung from the ceiling. Wolfgang's room

was the one after 314 and across from 315. The number on the door was 31. I figured that the 6 had fallen off. He swiped his card to open his door and led me in.

"You play Extreme Moto-X?" he asked.

"The video game? I used to."

It's a real old one. We don't have a system at home, but Jerry lets Raf and me play the ones in his shop.

"Take a seat." His voice was creaky, like a door that needed oiling. I guess he didn't talk much. He went to the TV for the controllers.

There was no seat. Just an unmade kid's bed, with a torn sticker of Daffy Duck on one side. The TV was on the far wall, maybe two paces from the bed. Not a big room.

The walls ran with damp. The air smelled sweet and rotten – unwashed clothes mixed with mildew and farts. I tried not to breathe too deep.

He plunked himself down on the bed and put my controller beside him. I sat cautiously. Had the sheets ever been changed?

Extreme Moto-X is a motorcycle race across a lame 2-D desert. The screen splits for two players. I was the bike on the left. I tried out the controller. Thumb-sized joystick, two buttons. B button was a skid control, I remembered. Okay then. I took a breath, shook my shoulders loose.

"The A button is jump, right?" I asked.

Wolfgang nodded, intent on the screen.

3—2—1—GO! The flag came down.

When the race started, the desert disappeared, replaced by my neighborhood. The graphics were a little better, and I recognized Wright Avenue west of Roncy, down the street from Wright Avenue Elementary School, where they might, at that very moment, be wondering where I was. (Or not. This wouldn't be the first day I'd skipped.)

I was expecting something like this to happen, but I got that stupid lump in my chest again. I never thought I was so emotional.

Like most streets in my neighborhood, Wright Avenue featured tall skinny houses leaning together, neat front lawns, cars parked like dominoes. My school was coming up on the north side – an old brick two-story. This was an early fall afternoon, the leaves just starting to turn color. Smelled like September. Fresh, you know? Even the dust smelled fresh.

I could see the back of another Moto-X cycle on my half of the screen. Wolfgang was ahead of me. Without thinking, I pushed the little joystick forward to accelerate. This was my past here – with my future on the line – but it was also a race. The bike skidded, so I pushed B to correct.

"Faster!"

I looked over. Wolfgang leaned forward, gripping his controller.

Fine. I'd show him. I pushed the joystick all the way forward and started to catch up. He swung left. I stayed straight, then saw I was about to hit a pothole. I pressed A, and the machine jumped in the air . . . and in a bump and a flash I was through the TV screen, careering down Wright on an *actual* Harley-Davidson Ironhead Chopper, neck and neck with Wolfgang.

I experienced a moment – a second really – of complete, total all-over awesomeness. Wow! Oh, wow! Then I saw the pothole coming up faster than I could steer. There was no A button on my motorcycle. I hit the middle of the pothole, lost control, and crashed the bike, flipping over the handlebars to land on the sidewalk in front of the school. Wolfgang stopped next to me and got off his bike, laughing at my spill. The moment he let go of his bike, it disappeared. Mine was gone too. Pretty cool, I thought. I got to my feet, unharmed. This was the past, after all. I wasn't really there.

We bounced toward the school like astronauts in zero g. Passing through the main floor window was as easy as pushing aside a curtain. We were in a classroom. "Grade one," said Wolfgang.

"I know."

We stayed at the back. It was the end of the day, and the kids were clustered on the carpet for story-time. I could smell the white glue, chalk, Magic Marker, and then, faint as hope, a whisper of perfumed soap. Miss Macrow's smell.

My first-grade teacher sat tall and straight in her story-time chair, holding the book so that the kids could see the pictures. She had long black hair and eyes like wet stones. Her dress went past her knees. Her hands were clean. Her voice had steel in it.

"What a bunch of losers!" sneered Wolfgang. Funny, coming from him. He was about the same age as the kids in this class.

I noticed a boy quietly picking his nose in the back

of the crowd. A big kid, with brown hair cut close and sloppy clothes. My grade-one self. He stared vacantly, not very interested in the story about the soldier who helped a witch find a tinderbox. He slid himself forward, rubbing his sock feet on the carpet to pick up static electricity. When he touched the bare neck of the little kid in front of him, there was a spark. The little kid started to cry. Jim smiled broadly.

Wolfgang nodded approvingly. "Nice going."

A lot of whispering and squirming on the story-time carpet now. A concerted movement, a general drawing away from the crying kid.

Is there someone in your life you hate for no reason? Their voice makes you want to throw up, their smile makes you want to punch it? Everything they do drives you crazy? You know someone like that? Me too. Lloyd. I hated his high pants and double-knotted running shoes. I hated his limp ginger hair and his long eyelashes. I hated the way he moved and talked. I hated the way he breathed.

He was the kid in front of Jim. His pale, round, first-grade face was squinched up, and his legs were twisted under him like a couple of pretzels. A stain darkened and spread across the story-time carpet underneath him.

Hey, Lloyd peed his pants! yelled Jim.

Lloyd closed his eyes.

Peed his pants, peed his pants. The class laughed.

"Is this why we're here?" I asked Wolfgang. "Is it Lloyd?"

"Huh?"

"Is *he* the one I'm supposed to remember?"

I was thinking back to what Tadeusz had said about these memories showing me who I should treat better. I still thought Lloyd was a ween, but I guess I had been a little mean to him. Wolfgang didn't know what I was talking about. He shrugged.

Quiet! Miss Macrow was on her feet. *Quiet, all of you!* She said all of you, but she was glaring at Jim. When he shuddered, I felt an echo of his fear myself. Wolfgang felt something too. He stopped laughing abruptly and put his thumb back in his mouth.

The beautiful, sweet-smelling, caring teacher knelt beside Lloyd and put her arms around him, ignoring the pee on the carpet, and Lloyd sniffed onto the sleeve of her blouse.

CHAPTER 10

The bell rang. We drifted out through the wall as easily as we'd drifted in. The fall afternoon was all around us, coating us with golden light. And here was Maq with his hair blowing all around his head. I'd recognized him back in class. He looked like a sunset from the neck up, had these big fat rays of red hair coming out from his head in all directions.

Maq walked home alone, even from grade one, because he lived next door to the school. He still lives there, but he switched to some genius school on the other side of the park, so I don't see him much anymore.

I heard a rhythmic banging sound behind us. I turned. Jim was pushing Lloyd against the back of a parked car. He had his hands on the smaller boy's shoulders, and he was slamming him into the rear bumper. *Bang. Bang. Bang.* This was happening between parked cars, hidden from the moms clustered in front of the school.

Wolfgang and I sat on the trunk of the nearer car. He nodded approvingly. "This takes me back," he said. "Good times. Good times."

He'd have been a tough, scary little kid, like Jim here. Like me.

Stop that!

Maq stood on the sidewalk with his hands on his hips. *Stop that at once!* he cried.

And now I remembered. "Oh, yeah," I said to Wolfgang. "I know what happens now."

Fighting is stupid. Stop now or I'll call my papa!

Jim threw Lloyd to the ground and stood over him, breathing hard. He had the dissatisfied, poison-ivy look. He'd scratched and felt better for two seconds, but the itch was back.

Are you calling me stupid? No one calls me stupid! said Jim. He stepped up onto the sidewalk, towering over Maq. Who didn't move.

Stupid! he cried.

They pushed back and forth for a few seconds. Jim punched Maq in the throat. Maq went down but climbed to his feet, roaring. He swung with his left hand, more push than punch because the arm was bent at the elbow. Jim grabbed the arm hard, and it came off in his hand. Yes, that's what I said. The whole arm, from well above the elbow, came away from Maq's body. His shirtsleeve flapped against the side of his chest.

You can see why I remember the scene.

For a second Jim stared at the arm, still bent at the elbow joint, a giant chicken wing. An actual arm, part of someone's body, and he'd ripped it away. I remember the shock, the feelings of power – and horror.

He screamed and dropped the arm.

Papa! cried Maq. *Papa, come quick!*

"Way to go!" Wolfgang nudged me. "Pick on the boy with one arm. Nice!"

"Hey, I didn't know the arm was fake." This was early in the year. I hadn't noticed that one of Maq's arms was always bent, and a slightly different color from the rest of his skin. Later on we got used to it. I remember Maq beating time in music class, clapping his living hand against the plastic one.

His dad came out on the porch. *What the hell is going on?* he shouted. He had a Montreal Canadiens accent, so it sounded like, *What de 'ell?* He was a barrel-chested guy in paint-stained overalls, with long dark hair and a beard. Looked a bit like a biker and a bit like Jesus. An old, fat Jesus. Had a big knobby nose on him.

    Maq! he shouted. *Where is your arm?*

    You know, you don't hear that question very often.

    Here, Papa. Maq picked it off the ground.

    Don't play games. Your arm is not a toy!

    This boy pulled it off!

    Maq's dad leapt down from the porch.

    Lloyd took off like a bullet from a gun, and Jim followed. I don't think either of them wanted to meet Maq's papa. As Wolfgang and I scrambled after them, I heard the man's deep laughter. Very genuine-sounding. Looking back, I saw him run up the steps with Maq under one arm and Maq's arm in his other hand. His big frame made the steps shudder. The front door slammed.

    Did I hear that laughter way back in grade one?

Back at the school, Lloyd was panting next to a man in a buttoned cardigan. The man sneezed, and Lloyd said, *Bless you, Daddy* in his piping voice. He was safe from Jim's bullying but still looked nervous. Cardigan Guy took his hand and led him down the street.

Jim was trying to explain things to Cassie and Louise. They'd have been in grade five. Louise was my sister's best friend. Still is. Chunky, average-looking, except for her chest. (You know how some girls are just enormous there? Louise looks like a map of Africa. I saw her in a bathing suit last week, tanning in the backyard with Cassie, and I had to run inside and take a shower. She was no more than ten or eleven here, and already she had something under her shirt.)

Where were you, Jim? called Cassie. *You were supposed to wait for me!*

Didn't you hear? I pulled off a guy's arm!

Cassie stamped her foot. *Jim!*

Really, I pulled and it came right off!

(It is funny, you know. Horrible, but funny too. No wonder Maq's dad had laughed.)

Wolfgang and I floated after the children like kites on strings. In the distance I could see the lake, glinting silver in the afternoon sun. On my left, the office towers of downtown poked their heads and shoulders above the blanket of trees and smog. I counted houses in from Roncesvalles. Mine was the fifth. One-half of the roof is green, the other gray. Raf and his dad move every year or two, but I've always lived in the same place.

I figured this was the end of the vision. I wondered about Maq and his dad. Should I apologize when I woke up in the hospital? Is that what Tadeusz wanted me to do? I hated apologizing.

We sank lower. Wolfgang was staring intently downward.

"Hey, there's Lloyd," I said. He and his dad were a few steps behind. I could hear snatches of their conversation.

. . . disappointed in you, said Lloyd's father.

Sorry, Daddy.

Sorry doesn't make a sandwich, son. You know that. Don't you? Don't you?

Lloyd's dad had a soft, sweet voice for yelling with. You'd never know he was mad. (Ma yells at me so loud she goes hoarse sometimes.) He was mad, though. He grabbed the back of his son's neck and twisted, bringing Lloyd's face around.

You crying?

No, sir. Wiping the tears away.

Oh, Lloyd.

I stopped noticing things at this point. Lloyd was crying, like his dad said, but – get this – the sound he made was *exactly* like that creepy mewing sound I'd heard Wolfgang do in the hotel lobby. Hearing it again, coming from Lloyd's mouth, transported me once more to the front seat of the big white Lincoln. Raf was busy under the steering column, and I was holding the flashlight. Midnight in a laneway full of garages. And things started to go wrong when I heard . . . I heard . . .

"Stop!" I said. "Stop!"

By an act of will, as sudden and non-reversible as leaping off a balcony, I wrenched my arm free of Wolfgang's grip. I dropped like a stone, landing with a thud . . . not on the sidewalk but on the grubby, damp, ill-smelling carpet in Wolfgang's hotel room. The Extreme Moto-X game was still on, but the screen was back to that 2-D desert. The video controller lay on the rug beside me.

CHAPTER 11

"You knew." I sat up.

"What?" Wolfgang leaned over to look down at me.

"You knew I hate cats. That's why you made that awful cat sound when you met me. Right?"

Sweat poured from his nose and chin, dripping onto the rug. It was like he was living in a private shower all the time. "I know what you're scared of," he said.

"How?" I stood. My heart and lungs were working overtime. Being scared takes it out of you. "How do you know I . . . don't like cats?"

Wolfgang sat back on the bed with his legs tucked under him and his thumb stuck deep in his mouth.

"I see you when I go back," he mumbled.

"Back? Back to Earth?"

He nodded solemnly, the way little kids can. On TV they look cute. Wolfgang looked about as cute as leprosy.

"Where do you see me?" I asked.

He didn't answer. He had gone all inward. His eyes were rolled up into his head.

"You're a Grave Walker, right?" I shook him. "Where do you see me when you come to Earth?"

I leaned over the bed. Wolfgang was sucking away on his thumb, eyes shut tight. Sweat beaded on his forehead, ran down his cheeks, soaked through his clothes and into the sheets. He rocked himself back and forth a few times. His breathing calmed down. He shuddered a couple of times, yawned, and began to breathe deeply. In minutes he was asleep.

Now what?

I had no idea what was supposed to happen next. Another indication that I was not dreaming this whole adventure. Dreams have a script of their own. There's no *Now what?* in a dream. Whatever the storyline – a road, a monster, a girl, a transformation, a flight through clouds of silver and gold – whatever is going on in your dream, on it goes with you in it. A dream is a river, and you have no more say about *where* you go than a floating twig.

I didn't want to stay in Wolfgang's room, so I left, closing the door quietly behind me. The elevator was empty. On my way down I noticed an advertising flyer peeling off the wall of the elevator. *Visit the Oasis on Four*. Why not? I thought. No reason to hang around the lobby. So when the elevator finally stopped, I pressed 4 and began wheezing and lurching my way back up.

Four was another cobwebby, dusty, bare-bulb-lit hallway. At the far end was a sign in burnt wood: *Oasis on Four*. Swinging double doors, like in an old west saloon. Smell of grease and smoke and despair. On my way I passed a door with *Cowgirls* on it. And beside it, *Cowboys*. Which reminded me . . .

———

I was in the hallway, wiping my hands on my pants, when the Cowgirl door opened and Marcie came out, grinning like a Halloween pumpkin.

"Hi!" She practically yelled it. "It's Jim, right? We met downstairs."

"Oh, yeah," I said. "Hi, Marcie. What are you doing up here?"

"Going to the bathroom, like you." She giggled.

I finished wiping my hands. "The Cowboy dryer is broken," I explained.

I didn't mean to make a joke, but she thought it was funny. She opened her face like a flower in the sun and laughed at me. Something about her. Her whole body vibrated from happiness. She was dancing even though she was standing still.

"I meant, what have you been doing?"

"Oh," she said wildly, "let's see. I watched a sad home movie with Raoul, and then I came up here. But while I was in the elevator something happened to my body down in the hospital. It turns out I'm going home early!"

She looked more like an elf than ever, her eyes lit with fire. I asked her what she was talking about.

"I'm in the hospital, remember? But Raoul says I'm coming out of my coma earlier than expected, so I'll wake up soon. I tell you, Jim, I can't wait. This place is *awful*."

Lowering her voice on the last word, as if she was afraid someone would overhear and be offended.

"I know." It was looking much better now than it had a moment ago, though. Looking at her, it was easy to forget my surroundings.

"Can you imagine staying here? Raoul says that a couple of the . . . *ghosts*," lowering her voice again, "have been here for hundreds of years! I'm so glad I'm going home."

"Raoul is the Mourner I saw you with down in the lobby? With the beard?"

"Yes. And so cold. Have you noticed how cold Mourners are? It's the sadness, I think. Raoul has such a sad story, Jim. Do you know he lost the only girl he ever loved at Wonderland? She wanted to go on the Crack-the-Whip coaster, and he didn't, so she went by herself, only something went wrong and the safety restraints on one side of the coaster released in the middle of a whip crack. Couples did okay, because the person with the working restraint could hang on to their partner, but all the people riding by themselves were flung out. Three of them died, and Raoul's girlfriend was one of them. He had a mouthful of nacho chips when he looked up and saw Desiree – that was her name – flying through the air. She landed on top of an Orange Julius stand and broke her neck. Raoul thought about her every day for the rest of his life. If only he'd gone on the ride with her, she'd be alive! He still can't eat nacho – What?"

She stared at me.

"Nothing."

"You were laughing?"

"No no," I said. "It's a sad story."

"You were so laughing. How can you do that, Jim? Poor Raoul."

"Poor Raoul," I echoed.

She knew I didn't mean it. After a second she smiled too. "Well, it was a long time ago," she said.

She put out her arms and spun around. Her dressing gown was open, and the hospital gown gaped for a second. She was wearing striped underpants. She saw me looking and blushed.

"Mom picked them," she said, tying her gown. "She thought they were cute."

"They are cute. Uh, I've got *Spider-Man* boxers today." My ma didn't pick them, though. I stole them from a department store downtown.

"What'll you do when you wake up from your coma?" I asked.

"I don't know. I guess I'll stay in the hospital for a few days and eat grapes. I think grapes are my favorite thing in the whole world." She grinned at me, like she was passing the ball. I passed it back. Now we were both grinning. "And then I'll go back to Galley Avenue. Scipio will be so happy to see me."

Galley Avenue crosses Roncesvalles a block below my house. The girl lived around the corner from me.

"Who's Scipio?" I asked. "A boyfriend?"

Everything I said made her laugh. She killed herself over this one. "Scipio's my dog. I don't have a boyfriend."

I laughed too. We stopped laughing at the same time and stared at each other.

"I don't have a girlfriend," I said.

"No, eh?"

"Never had one."

"Really?"

She took a step toward me. Her face was level with mine. Pale bluish shadows under her eyes.

"Really."

"You're nice, Jim."

"Who, me?"

"When I first saw you, I thought you looked mean."

"You're talking about down in the lobby? When you came in? You noticed me then?"

"Yeah. You were sitting on the stairs."

I may have blushed. Probably did. "I was watching you," I said. "I didn't think you were looking at me."

"Well, I was. That red shirt stood out in this awful gray place. I thought you looked mean, but I was wrong."

"No, no. I am kind of mean." I made a face. "*Grrr.* See?"

She laughed harder than ever, then darted forward like a dancer, put her hands on my shoulder, and kissed me on the cheek.

I can still feel the print of her lips.

She pulled away fast. "I don't do that a lot," she said. "But I couldn't help it, Jim. You looked so cute, growling like that, and I'm so . . . so . . ." She waved her arms.

"Crazy," I said.

"Yes. Crazy with happiness." She laughed like anything and then, all of a sudden, started to cry.

CHAPTER 12

The elevator made that *ding* noise, and Tadeusz stepped out into the hallway.

"Jim!" he whispered. His face didn't light up or anything, but he seemed pleased. "Great to see you. You must be here for your third vision."

"I am?"

"Sure. Didn't I tell you, down on Roncy? Three memories, three ghosts. You've had two so far. This will be your third. How are you doing?"

"Um, okay," I said.

I was taken aback. Here I thought I was acting independently, and it turned out I was following a script all along.

Tadeusz was carrying a net bag full of small fruit. Limes, they looked like, except they were gray.

He started to introduce himself to Marcie, but she interrupted. "I know who you are, Mr. Kosinski," she said, wiping her eyes. "I recognize you."

Her voice had gone all cold.

"Call me Tadeusz, please," he said.

She shook her head. "Mr. Kosinski. That's what you told my mom to call you when you kicked us out of our house."

Tadeusz took a step back. "No," he said. "Oh, *no*. Did I –"

"Two years ago. We lived in the back part of a house on Fermanagh. My mom lost her job at the tax department and couldn't pay the rent. You told her we had to leave. She was about to start a new job at a bakery. She promised to pay double next month. You said no. Do you remember now?"

I must say, it sounded like him. He was famous up and down Roncy as a tough young businessman.

Tadeusz hung his head. "Yes," he moaned. "Yes, I do."

"I came to the door when I heard my mom crying. I was twelve years old. Had a puppy in my arms. There was a moving truck parked in the laneway behind our house. My mom was begging you. 'Please, Tadeusz,' she said. And you told her to call you Mr. Kosinski."

"Stop," he said. "Please stop."

He had his hands clasped together, like he was praying.

"If you are interested, Mr. Kosinski, my mom is now a shift manager at the bakery. We live in a whole house now. Our backyard has a water feature, and our landlord is putting down new carpeting for us."

Tadeusz swallowed. "I am sorry for what I did to you. So sorry."

He could not meet her eyes. I felt bad for him.

Please don't let this happen to me, I thought. Please don't let me turn into Tadeusz.

An enormous crash made the whole hallway shake. Dust fell from the ceiling.

"What was that?" I asked.

"Morgan."

"Who's he?"

"You'll find out. You'll meet him."

"Does Morgan stay here?" asked Marcie.

"Of course. He's stuck like everyone else here. Only he's not a Mourner, like me or Raoul."

Another bone-jarring thud. The Cowgirl sign fell off the bathroom door.

"Is he a Grave Walker?" I asked. I hoped not. I didn't want to meet anyone like Wolfgang.

"No no. No. Fear has no hold on Morgan. He's a Slayer."

I heard a roaring sound, like a . . . I don't know, a bull or something. Marcie shivered and reached for my hand.

Not fear or sadness. I wondered what emotion Slayers felt. A Slayer was a kind of killer. Could that tie you to Earth?

Raoul, Marcie's Mourner, appeared in the doorway a moment later. He was side on to us, and at first I thought he was floating. His feet were off the floor and he was twisting his skinny body around. "Put me down!" he said.

Then I saw the arm that held Raoul's shirtfront. Someone was holding him in the air.

A giant. A storm cloud. A fire. A demon. These images passed through my mind when I saw Morgan for the first time. He filled the doorway and gave off a blast of heat that shot down the hall, making me blink. He tossed

Raoul away when he caught sight of us and opened his mouth wide, showing teeth that had been filed to points.

"Hellfire!" he cried.

He was dressed like someone off the History Channel – high boots, belt, and a kerchief to keep his long hair out of his eyes. Everything was gray, of course, but he wasn't like the other ghosts I'd met. His voice boomed and echoed like a gong.

He came down the hall with a rolling, swaggering walk. The heat intensified. He was a furnace. We shrank back.

He snatched the bag of limes from Tadeusz. "About time!" he cried. "I've been waiting for these!"

He grabbed my shoulder.

"Can you make grog, kid?" he said.

I didn't know what grog was. I shook my head. His hand was burning me.

"You'd better be a hellfire quick learner," he said. And dragged me down the hall.

"Marcie!" My voice cracked.

"Shut up, kid!"

"Marcie! I'll look for you when I get back! What's your address? What's your last name?"

I couldn't see her past Morgan's shoulder. I didn't hear her reply.

CHAPTER 13

The Oasis was a long room. The bar was on the left-hand side as you went in. There were booths on the other side and a pool table at the back.

Morgan dragged me behind the bar, dropped me like a sack of laundry, and told me to start cutting limes. Apparently you need them to make grog. Also sugar, rum, hot water, and cinnamon. I did the work: measuring, boiling, mixing, pouring the hot smelly drink into a pitcher. Morgan sat on a barstool and told me to go faster.

The floor was covered in broken glass. Every now and then Morgan would kick a piece of glass away from him. I had wondered before how this hotel worked. Was the place ever cleaned? Were the vending machines ever refilled? Would anyone sweep up this glass?

Man, I did *not* want to end up here.

There was a small TV behind the bar, tuned to the local news. I recognized the anchor. Looking at her, you knew that the headlines were important and sexy.

Morgan downed his drink, frowned, and banged down his glass.

"Hellfire! That was awful!" he cried. "Worst grog I ever had. Now do me another one."

I lifted the pitcher, poured carefully.

"More, damn it!" he called. "Right to the rim!"

I smiled. I was getting used to his style. Reminded me of people I knew. I was even getting used to the glow coming from him. It was like living under a heat vent.

"Don't make faces, kid. You're not here for play acting."

He reached for the remote.

My third vision started on a gray afternoon in the crappy time of year between Halloween and Christmas, when the trees are bare, the sun goes down early, and there's no snow. Jim was walking down Roncesvalles, smoking a cigarette, which made him look pretty stupid. Oh well. Morgan and I floated after him.

"How'd we get inside the TV picture?" I asked.

"Who cares, kid? We're here."

He had his glass in his free hand. Took a sip.

"But it happened so fast," I said. "How did it happen so fast?"

He hawked and spat. "This is your third time, right? So maybe you're getting better at going back to the past. Now shut up and watch."

Jim wore a black bomber-style jacket and mitts. I wore that jacket up until last year, even though it was getting too small for me by then.

We floated above the Krakow Restaurant. Morgan spat again. I watched the droplets of spittle disappear into the gray afternoon. I wondered if he was spitting here in the vision or in the Oasis lounge too.

Jim took a drag, threw away the butt, turned down Garden Avenue. He must have been to the Buy and Sell after school. Jerry used to hand out cigarettes.

We reached the house. Morgan and I drifted down like dandelion fluff across the front porch and through the front window into the living room. Cassie was sitting on the couch watching *Oprah*.

Jim grabbed the remote from his sister and fell onto the couch. She tried to take it back, but he held her off.

Give it back! she said. *Or I'll make you wish you had.*

No, said Jim, his voice breaking. The word began as a squeak and ended as a croak. So embarrassing to be a boy, sometimes.

Cassie laughed. *No-oo? What does No-oo mean?*

You shut up!

He pointed the remote, and Oprah's face turned into Yosemite Sam's. Jim sat back and watched as the little man with the big mustache chased Bugs Bunny up a ladder. Underneath was a swimming pool with alligators in it. In the background a busy piano played, *Deedly deedly dee, dee, dee.*

"This is a great cartoon," I told Morgan. I floated over behind the couch so I could see the TV better. When Yosemite Sam said that he'd paid his four bits for the high-diving act and that he was going to see the high-diving act, I mouthed the words along with him.

Cassie worried at a fingernail, watching Jim sidelong.

Yosemite Sam lost his balance on the diving board, teetered, and fell. Jim and I laughed together, and Cassie lunged for the TV remote. Jim transferred it to his other hand and held it away from her. Now she swarmed over him, grabbing with both hands and crying out.

Ma! Jim is bugging me!

Am not!

She peered intently past his head, looking at nothing. Well, actually, she was looking right at me and Morgan, but of course she couldn't see us. The remote was still out of her reach.

"Oh, yeah," I said as my dozing memory finally woke up. "I know what's going to happen now." I tried to look away but found I couldn't. I guess when you're remembering something you have to remember it.

Morgan yawned, showing his mixed mouthful of dirty, pointy teeth.

Cassie bent her head gracefully, grabbed her brother's shoulders, and kneed him in the groin. Hard. He screamed. I groaned. Even the shadow of the pain hurt.

You won't need to take a long shower today, Jim, she laughed.

"Quite a vixen, your sis." Morgan finished his drink and tossed the glass away from him. It disappeared.

The remote fell from Jim's hands and bounced on the dirty rug. Cassie scrambled for it, like some large insect, all legs and arms. On-screen, Yosemite Sam was being eaten by alligators.

Jim lay on the couch, hunched over and breathing hard. *Oprah* was back on, but Cassie wasn't watching. She danced over to me and stared right into my eyes. She put her hand out. I moved away, like we were playing blind man's bluff. She followed me. Fear, excitement, and a kind of specialness in her face.

Peek-a-boo, I see you, she whispered. *You're dead, aren't you, Jim?*

CHAPTER 14

"She can see us," I said to Morgan. "How can she see us?"

"How in hellfire do I know?"

"It doesn't make sense," I said. "This is my past, right?"

"Yes, but you aren't the only one in it. It is your sis's past too. You're not replaying a memory here, you lackwit! This is what really happened."

"But how can Cassie see ghosts? Is she hallucinating? Is there a physical explanation?"

"Why do you want to know so much, kid?"

He sounded like Cap now. *"I want to know" can get you in trouble, Jim.*

I turned back to Cassie. She was still talking to us. *How old are you, Jim – thirteen?* she said. *Fourteen, maybe. Not much older than now. Wow. And who's your friend? He looks cool. Does he kill you? Is that how you die?*

I remembered all the times that Cassie had weirded me out, staring into corners, talking to people who weren't there. Turned out they were there all along. No wonder she'd panicked when she saw my dragon shirt at breakfast. (*You're dead! That's your dead shirt.*)

Morgan shot at her with his finger. She shot him back.

———

Ma came downstairs in a housecoat with a headache, wincing at every step. Her eyes were almost closed.

What's all the racket? she said.

Cassie hurt me, said Jim. *And now she's in the corner talking to invisible people again. Make her stop.*

Ma exhaled like a deflating tire. *Both of you stop. Stop everything!* She walked right past us to get to the kitchen.

"Someone's got a hangover," said Morgan.

Jim was like an open gasoline can looking for a match. There was nowhere to put his anger. Oh, did I remember that feeling. He went out, slamming the front door. I wanted to talk to Cassie, but when it was just us and Oprah in the room, I found I couldn't stay. A giant hand pulled at me. I was outside before I knew it, following Jim down Garden Avenue toward High Park. He stomped along, shoulders twitching under his bomber jacket, kicking at stones and swearing to himself. When he came to the mailbox at the corner of Garden and Indian Road, he pushed it over. It made a satisfactory booming sound when it hit the sidewalk.

A sour old lady watched him from down the street with a frown of deep disapproval. She carried a cane and wore glasses and thick shoes. *Hooligan!* she called.

Jim whirled around, his face a stain of rage. The old lady walked forward gamely, her legs moving like crooked pistons.

Knocking over a mailbox! Aren't you ashamed of yourself?

He growled at her. Honestly, like an animal. Even the echo of my past rage was impossible for me to ignore. I could feel anger rising in me like hot water in a bath. I wanted to punch the old lady almost as much as Jim did.

Morgan nodded.

"I know, kid," he said. "Orlanda drives me crazy too."

Orlanda? That's right, it was the lady from the front desk of the hotel. She must have recognized me – which would explain why she'd glared at me on the way in. Here she was in my past.

Would Jim actually have punched her? I don't know. He wanted to. But at that moment the parked car beside him came to life with a cough and a rumble, and an extremely familiar head popped up from the driver's side of the front seat. Jim's scowl dissolved into a grin.

Hey, Rafal, what are you doing here?

Raf leaned across to open the passenger-side door.

Want to come for a ride, Jim?

'Kay.

The anger melted inside me. Jim got in. Morgan and I drifted through the rear fender into the backseat. The motor roared, and the car spun away from the curb. Rafal steered up Sunnyside and along High Park Boulevard to the park itself, about a million acres of green in the west end of the city. The dashboard clock said 5:17. The park gates were open. We drove in.

Rafal is my best friend, even though he's a year older than me and goes to high school. He's short and wide but tough with it, all corners. He almost always has a grin on. I remember him fighting with Sparks once, in the back room at Jerry's. Sparks is bigger and stronger, must have knocked Raf down a dozen times, but Raf kept bouncing back onto his feet, smiling like anything. Sparks got so upset he grabbed a bowling ball out of a box of junk and threw it. A bowling ball! It was the first thing he could put his hand on. Raf ducked and the ball smashed a window. (Jerry kicked Sparks out of the shop for a week. Crazy but cool, that's Raf. *Never let them see you mad*, he says. *When my old man is hitting me, I just smile. Drives him bananas.*)

Thinking about Rafal made me feel awful. What had happened to him last night? What had I done?

Back to the memory. There's a network of lanes running through High Park. Raf pulled off to the side near the main gates and asked Jim if he wanted to drive. Jim's eyes lit up like fireworks. They traded places, clambering over each other and laughing. When Jim put his foot down, the car stalled. He went to restart it, but there wasn't a key. A tangle of ignition wires hung down from under the steering column.

You boosted this car! said Jim.

Rafal's eyes quirked up. His grin was sudden and vivid, fork lightning in the night sky. He took a flashlight from the pocket of his ski jacket and fiddled under the dashboard.

"You start with the ignition wires," I explained to Morgan from the backseat. "Strip the ends and connect them. There'll be a shock, but . . ."

"This isn't my past, kid," he said. "I don't give a damn."

When the dash lights came on, Raf turned to the starter wires, connecting red to brown. There was a spark and the engine turned over. Since the car was in gear when it stalled, it kicked forward.

Give her some gas! Raf shouted.

'Kay!

Jim steered into the park. The autumn twilight was spooky. Deep shadows, dark colors, a sense of foreboding. Bare tree branches met overhead, like clasped fingers. A lonely kid trudged ahead of us. The cloth overcoat flapped around his bony figure. His hair blew in the wind.

I know that guy, Jim told Raf. *And I hate him.*

Then . . . give her some more gas! shouted Raf.

Jim sped up and aimed the car right at Lloyd. I could feel his anger running like flame through my own body. I know how this scene ended. I didn't run Lloyd down, but . . . was I trying to? Or was I maybe using him as a way to get back at Cassie? It occurred to me that this last vision had had a lot of anger in it.

Lloyd had seen the car now, but he hadn't got out of the way. He stood, poised between fears – which way to jump?

Morgan was leaning forward in the seat. "Exfluncticate the boy!" he shouted, shaking a rough scarred fist. His other hand went to the hilt of his cutlass. "Exfluncticate him!"

A raccoon ambled into the road ahead of us, hump-backed and heedless. Raf grabbed the wheel, pulled it down. The car jumped the curb and crashed into the underbrush on the near side of the road.

(So that's how it happened! I knew I'd crashed the car, but the details were hazy.)

The air was full of noise. Jim and Raf were shouting. Branches knocked against the windows as we rushed past. *Foot off the gas!* Raf said. And then my name, over and over. *Jim! Jim! Jim!*

"Jim!"

Tadeusz's voice. I blinked. High Park, Raf, the stolen car, and my past had vanished. I was back behind the Oasis bar, smelling lime and cinnamon and treading on broken glass. Morgan and Tadeusz stood across the bar from me. The TV was back on the news channel.

"Time to go, Jim," said Tadeusz.

I breathed a sigh of relief. The place was starting to get to me. It was so very full of unhappiness.

"Great!" I said. "I can't wait to get out of here." I was thinking of what I'd do when I got back home. The changes I'd make. The people I'd be better to, so that I'd never ever ever *ever* run the risk of ending up back here when I finally did die.

Morgan laughed so hard he spilled his drink.

"What's so funny?"

Tadeusz clasped his hands in front of him and looked at the floor.

"*What?*" I said.

"I've got horrible news, Jim," he said.

CHAPTER 15

"I'm *what?*"

"Dying," said Tadeusz. He was looking at me now. Big, fat concerned expression, which went so oddly with his wise-guy suit. He needed a shave.

"But you said I *wasn't* dying. Remember? You didn't say anything about dying – just told me to pay attention. And I've been doing that."

"You were supposed to wake up in the hospital. But something is going wrong down on the street. Your body is reacting badly."

"What do you mean, reacting badly?" I was talking fast now. "How badly? What's wrong with my body?"

"I don't know, Jim. I'm not –"

"You don't *know?*"

"I'm not a –"

"You're a *ghost*, Tadeusz. You're immortal. You know the future enough to warn people. What's wrong with me?"

"I'm not a doctor," said Tadeusz calmly. "All I know is what I hear from the front desk. It seems that your vital signs have suddenly started dropping and that you are going to die soon. I'm very sorry."

"I feel fine," I said to Tadeusz. "Same as I did when I arrived."

"Sorry," he said again.

Morgan snorted.

"You shut up!" I told him. I leaned over the bar and knocked the drink out of his hand. But that only made him laugh harder. "Hellfire!" he cried. "Aren't you an angry sunket?" He bent to retrieve the glass.

I wanted something to focus on. There was a framed photograph on the wall behind the bar. Cowboy, cowgirl, horse. The three of them looked like they belonged together. They were natural, regular folks – and yet special too, with their hats and guns and stuff. They were like a perfect family. I squinted to read the writing at the bottom of the photo. *Happy trails to you . . .*

I turned back to Tadeusz. "So . . . will I get a chance to change? The whole point of me coming here for the day was so I could learn stuff. Pay attention, you said. And I have! I know I'm a piece of crap, just like Denise said. I'm full of sadness, and fear. I've let a bunch of people down. I've been angry and mean. But I want to change. I don't want to be a piece of crap anymore. I want to say sorry to Maq and Lloyd. And Raf. I want to see Marcie again. I want to talk to Cassie!"

I came around the bar and put my hand on his cold arm. "Please, Tadeusz. I don't want to die now. I don't want to end up here. I don't . . ."

I stopped. I was staring at my hand. Was it my imagination or had my skin changed color? I am not a dark guy, don't take much of a tan. But I had never seen my hand so pale, so silvery, so . . . gray. Was the dragon shirt as bright as it had been? To be honest, it looked a little faded.

No. No. No!

"How much time do I have?" I asked Tadeusz.

"Not much."

"Hours? Minutes? Do I have time to talk to anyone? You know Cassie actually saw me and Morgan as ghosts! I'd like a chance to talk to her. Or Marcie." I was panicking, thinking of all the people I wanted to see.

He shook his head.

"Please, Tadeusz! Please. One minute with Marcie. That's not much to ask? Do it for a fellow Roncesvaller. A guy from the old neighborhood!"

"Jim," he said gently, "everyone here is from the old neighborhood."

Morgan tossed his empty glass in the bar sink, where it rattled around.

"Come on, kid." He got to his feet. "Let's go."

"You?" I said. "You're going with me?"

"Hellfire! Of course I'm going with you. I wouldn't miss it."

He belched.

"I need to be there," he said.

I remembered how Denise was drawn to her son by her own regret. How Wolfgang was drawn to Lloyd's fear by his own.

Morgan was tied to Earth too.

I waved to Tadeusz from the doorway.

"Good-bye, Jim."

Morgan pushed me into the hall. His hand on my back felt like a blow. "Good-bye, huh?" he said. "More like *Au revoir!*"

In the elevator on the way down, I thought, *I'm dying.* I thought, *I'm dying.* I thought, *I'm actually dying.* I thought, *Crap crap crap.*

Orlanda was still at the front desk. She took my day pass and pursed her lips at me. "Not so very colorful as you were, Jim," she said.

I felt anger sloshing around inside me. She leaned closer, so that I felt the cool self-satisfaction coming off her skin.

"Not so snooty, are you? You remind me of a whipped puppy."

"Yeah, well, you remind me of SHUT UP!"

The words popped out before I could stop them. An instinctive reaction. Too bad, because this would have been a perfect opportunity for me to apologize for being sort of mean to her about the mailbox.

Orlanda's mouth had dropped open like an oven door. I tried to smooth things over and show how I had changed.

"Nice, uh, tonsils," I said. "So clean and shiny. You must be very proud."

Idiot!

Morgan dragged me to the door, kicked it open.

"You told *her*," he said. "Reminds me of shut up. Ha! That was the beatenest thing."

I sighed.

After the horrid drab gray of the hotel, the sky looked like it had just been washed. So bright it hurt my eyes.

"Ready to die, kid?"

"It just seems so *unfair* to me, you know?"

"Well, it seems SHUT UP to me." A wide grin. "Did you smoke that? Like what you said to Orlanda? You'd make a cat laugh."

He stepped into space, dragging me after him.

CHAPTER 16

We dropped like stones. So much faster than the way I had gone up with Denise. Looking down was like one of those satellite projection shots that start with Earth from space and end up with a view of the inside of your mouth where gingivitis germs are giving you bad breath. In our case, the shot steadied and slowed when we were approaching street level. A traffic jam stretching up and down Roncesvalles. Two police cars blocked the intersection at Wright Avenue. Between them stood an ambulance with open rear doors. Morgan and I dropped onto street level, joining the crowd of gapers, chatters, yawners, and tsk-tskers.

The paramedics were rolling a stretcher toward the ambulance. Morgan and I moved closer. No one could see us, and yet people got out of our way. Maybe they felt Morgan's heat. One woman took out a handkerchief and mopped her face as we passed.

It was my body on the stretcher, all right. My shirt, my blood-stained face.

I wanted to shake my unconscious self awake. I wanted to fight someone. I wanted to cry.

I could hear people in the crowd asking one another what happened. They weren't all speaking English, but I knew what they were saying anyway. It was like I was watching a dubbed film. (Seriously cool. Too bad there were no ninjas. I love those films.)

I saw Cap and Sparks standing on the edge of the crowd, sipping coffee from paper cups, laughing together. Not very nice guys.

Mr. K from the fruit store stood near me, gabbling away to an old Korean lady from a corner store a few blocks away.

I KNOW THAT BOY, he said. I SEE HIM EVERY DAY, HE IS A NO GOOD ONE. HE ROBS MY PLACE OF BUSINESS. I HATE HIM. He talked in the strange formal way of dubbed films. It was funny to see his lips moving out of sequence with what I heard him say.

The old lady nodded her gray head. I KNOW AND HATE HIM ALSO, she said. HE IS A SON OF UNMARRIED PARENTS.

The two paramedics wore dark blue uniforms. Short sleeves showed off their meaty arms. They lifted the stretcher into the back of the ambulance and transferred the body over to a bench that took up most of one side. The clean-shaven one climbed through to the driver's seat.

"Come on," said Morgan.

"What do you mean?"

"What the hellfire do you think I mean? Come on." And he picked me up in one hand and carried me into the ambulance.

I saw Mr. K through the open doors. He stood at the front of the crowd. His face was a mask, expressionless, all his life hidden behind his eyes.

DO YOU THINK THE BOY IS BADLY HURT? he said.

MAYBE HE IS DEAD, said the lady with him.

They nodded solemnly at each other. Mr. K's apron flapped around his bony figure like a flag around a pole.

GOOD! he said, though his lips kept moving for a while after the word came out.

The paramedic with the luxuriant mustache closed the doors. The ambulance inched past the cop cars, turned down Wright Avenue, and picked up speed.

I thought back to all the times I'd stolen fruit and laughed at Mr. K.

Mustache was on the phone.

"Yeah, darlin', this is Bill. And how are you this fine afternoon? Excellent. Listen, we have a road accident here. Unconscious teen with head trauma and some respiratory distress. Pulse weak. Yeah, serious. We'll be on your doorstep in about ten minutes. Right? Thanks, darlin'. You're a princess. No, I'm not kidding, you really are. Yes you are. How do I know? Because your mama is the Queen. That's her on the twenty, isn't it? Sure it is."

We were flying along Wright, the siren loud enough to rattle the garbage can lids.

Morgan couldn't get enough of Jim. He watched him intently, nudging me whenever Jim twitched or choked.

"He's dying," I said. "Leave him alone."

"Yes, dying." Morgan clenched both fists. "And he doesn't want to. He's fighting! His whole body is going crazy to stay alive. Heart, liver, lights, tripe, blood and boiling, roly-poly, gammon, and spinach – everything in him is working double tides, sweating and straining. I've seen thousands die, and it's always the same. No one goes easy, kid. No one. Look!"

He pointed at Jim's throat.

"There's the battle. He's fighting with every nerve and sinew, each breath a victory! It's a shambles in there, kid. And all that struggle is in vain. The enemy is stronger. The enemy is always stronger. The boy is fighting, but he's going to lose. You're going to lose."

Morgan's nostrils flared. He inhaled deeply.

I couldn't help noticing how pale my skin looked. I was definitely washed out. My clothes too – I could hardly tell what color my shirt was anymore, it was so faded.

Crap crap crap.

CHAPTER 17

For a few minutes, nothing much happened. You ever feel sick to your stomach, run to the toilet to throw up, lean over, and . . . nothing? It was like that. The horror didn't go away – it just got put on hold for a bit. Jim lay on the bench trying to breathe. Morgan watched him closely. Bill the paramedic called forward to ask if Bucky felt as hot as he did. I tried not to hope. It was hard. Yes, everyone had told me I was dying. The evidence lay in front of me – my body in an ambulance, in a coma. But I couldn't help thinking, What if I lived after all? What if Jim's insides somehow turned the battle around? Miracles sometimes happened. Also, and I am not proud of this, I found myself getting distracted. Dying did not concentrate my mind. I wanted to know things.

"What are you doing here?" I asked Morgan. "Did you live around Roncy, like Tadeusz and Denise?"

"No."

The siren whooped. We slowed to a crawl to pass through a busy intersection and took off again. Bill wiped his forehead on his short sleeve.

"I called nowhere home when I was alive," said Morgan. "I sailed the seven seas, Halifax to the Mauritius, China to Peru, with only the width of a plank between me and eternity. And I have been drifting ever since, inn to inn, hotel to hotel, wherever I can find what I . . . need." His jaw went rigid for a moment. I waited for more, but he didn't go on.

"How long ago was that?" I asked. "When did you die?"

He bared his saw teeth in an animal grimace. "Seventeen twenty. And I didn't die – I was murdered by my own captain, the foulest, most treacherous pirate who ever flew the flag of blood."

Morgan had large hands. When he clenched them into fists, the knuckles bulged like walnuts.

"You were a *pirate*?" I gaped. "You kind of dress like one, I guess, but I never . . . I mean, I thought it was just that. . . . You mean you really *were* a pirate? Like Jack Sparrow, or Captain Hook? They are *so* cool."

"I was no captain," he said bitterly. "Edward Low captured my fishing boat off the Carolinas. I joined his crew and did what I was told."

"I never heard of Edward Low," I said.

"Name him *not*!"

Morgan's jaws snapped together. He grabbed me by the throat. "That devil stole my life. And not mine alone. He cut off Thomas Cocklyn's lips and ears. He flogged Sam Bellamy for an hour after he was dead. He shot me in the back for no reason. 'If I didn't shoot one of you now and then, you'd forget me,' he said."

It wasn't regret or fear that had tied him to Earth for three hundred years. And it sure wasn't love of battle. It was rage. He craved the violence of death. He needed to be here. His hands on my neck felt like a collar of fire.

I struggled to pull them away. "You're choking me," I whispered.

He stared at me hungrily.

"I can't breathe," I said. "You're killing me."

He spoke then. "I'm a Slayer," he said. "It's what I do."

I panicked, kicking and twisting, but still couldn't get air into my lungs. My head flopped sideways, and I saw Jim thrashing around on the bench. He couldn't breathe either.

Darkness gathered around me and rose to cover me. I sank into it with a silent scream. Anyone who says dying is easy has never tried it.

Bill the paramedic was talking. His voice echoed strangely in my head, like an announcement at a train station.

"What's our ETA at St. Mike's, Bucky?" he called out.

"Five minutes. Maybe six."

"Damn."

"What's wrong?"

"Patient's asphyxiating. Looks like another DOA."

The siren whooped in the background.

I lay on my back, on the bench. I was Jim now, the body. I saw Bill take a sterile package from a drawer and peel it open. On the other side of the ambulance I saw Morgan with his hands round the neck of my ghost, that pathetic struggling piece of crap.

I did *not* want to die and spend a gray eternity between Roncy and the Jordan Arms. I wanted another chance.

Seconds left to live. Seconds. I couldn't breathe in, but there was enough air left in my lungs for one word. I forced a word out.

"Help!" I cried from the bench.

Seconds.

I don't know if Bill heard my cry, but Morgan did. He looked over at me, the body. My ghost took this opportunity to thumb him hard in the eye.

"Hellfire!"

Morgan let go. Bill swabbed my throat with alcohol and cut deep with the X-Acto knife he'd taken from the sterile package. A thin stream of air reached my lungs. Morgan swore again. Bill was still working, feeding a length of narrow tubing into my throat. Another breath, easier this time. And another.

Morgan floated near me, scowling deeply, tearing from one eye. My ghost had disappeared. I was going to live.

I smiled and closed my eyes. When I opened them, I was in a hospital bed with a headache the size of Lake Erie.

PART TWO

ME DOING A LITTLE BETTER

CHAPTER 18

I tried to speak. Couldn't. My throat felt like sandpaper. I tried to say, Where am I? and it came out like, *Wahmmaaaam.* No one answered.

The light in my eyes made my headache worse. I tried to say, Put out the light, and it came out like, *Pahlaaaaa.* No one did anything.

I turned away. No I didn't. Red hot spikes in the back of my head stopped me from moving.

I fell asleep.

Next time I woke up things started coming into focus. I was in a hospital bed, surrounded by bloops and gurgles and whooshing noises. A nurse stood by my bed. "Good morning, Jim," she said loudly.

Light in my eyes again. My nurse moved it around. I followed it with my eyes. "Very good," she said.

My hands were tied to my sides. I started to wonder why and then fell asleep.

Next time I woke up, an old lady was sitting next to me, squeezing my tied hand.

"Jim," she said. "Oh, Jim."

"Ma," I said. My lips felt like balloons. My throat burned.

My tied left hand hurt when she squeezed it.

"Ouch. Let go," I said.

"Oh, Jim," she said again. She couldn't understand me. It was her, all right. Smoke-gruff voice, face like a crumpled fender. Ma. I was happy to see her.

"What happened?" I asked. "How'd I get here?"

"Oh, Jim," she said.

I went back to sleep.

A doctor shook me awake and asked me questions. Name, address, how many fingers. I told her.

"Good," she said.

Her name was Dr. Driver. She untied me.

My throat still hurt. I reached up, but the doc grabbed my arm in midair.

"No, Jim," she said. "Let your throat alone. You had a tube sticking out of there, but it's gone. Now you have to let the wound heal."

She asked me to make a fist, touch my fingers together. I did them easy enough, except that there was a needle and a tube coming out of my right wrist and they got in the way.

"Good," she said again.

There was another bag below the bed, with a tube attached to my dick. Pretty gross.

The doc was real old, maybe like fifty. She had a white coat, glasses, and her gray hair in a ponytail. Her lips were a thin line. She took a microphone from her pocket and started asking me about the last thing I remembered before waking up in the hospital.

"What about the accident?" she asked. "Do you remember that?"

"I remember a car," I said.

"Go on."

"Big white car. A Lincoln."

"I don't know about the car that hit you."

"Raf was with me. It was dark."

She frowned. I shut up. Just in time I remembered that we were inside the Lincoln, boosting it. I wasn't going to talk into a microphone about that.

"What do you remember after the Lincoln?"

"I went home." The doc nodded encouragement. "I was wearing a new shirt."

"New shirt. Good. Go on, Jim."

But I couldn't. I tried, but my memory was a pocket with a hole in it. There was nothing there after the Lincoln.

I caught myself trying to touch my throat. "Did I really have a tube sticking out here?" I asked. You know, that would look kind of cool, walking down the street with a tube out your throat. Hold a cigarette up to it, take a drag, let the smoke out.

All right, maybe not too cool. But interesting.

"You started to choke in the ambulance, and the paramedic stuck a tube in so you could breathe," said Dr. Driver. "Do you remember that?"

It hurt to shake my head.

"You're a lucky guy, Jim. You could have died in the ambulance, or later on the operating table. Blood clots near the brain are tricky. But you came through. It's incredible, really. There's a lot we don't understand."

"How long have I been here?" I asked.

She checked my chart. "Admitted Tuesday after-noon, and it's Friday now. That's three days."

"Was I in a coma?"

"Yes."

"Comas are cool."

She shook her head.

"You'll be leaving the Intensive Care Unit soon. We'll keep you in the hospital a while longer, make sure you can move on your own before we let you go home. Your mother says you're twelve years old – is that right?"

"I'm fourteen."

"I thought you looked bigger than twelve. I've got a twelve-year-old at home. In fact, you look pretty big for fourteen."

She waited a sec, then said casually, "Your mother doesn't visit very often, Jim. You two get on okay?"

I shrugged. "Not bad."

"It's just that most moms practically live here when their kids are sick. What about the rest of your family – dad, grandparents, brothers and sisters. Are they in the picture?"

I told her I had a sister. "But I don't think she's any-where near the picture," I said.

"Oh," said the doc.

Next time I woke up I was in a regular room, with a mean nurse and a geezer roommate named Chester who wheezed.

The nurse showed me how to walk, pushing around a clear plastic bag on a pole. First trip was to the bathroom down the hall. (I didn't have a tube attached to my dick anymore.) She left me alone but came busting in when I screamed.

I was staring into the mirror. First time I'd seen myself since the accident. "I'm bald!" I cried.

"They shaved you for the operation," the nurse told me. "Stop whining, you baby. It'll grow back."

Ma came to visit once but didn't stay. I was on the fifth floor. That was a lot of up and down for her. I told her I was glad to see her.

"Are you?"

"Yeah."

She coughed a couple of long, rumbly ones. Sounded like an old car starting in the rain.

"Can I ask you something then, Jim?"

"Yeah."

I was sitting up in bed with my knees raised under the covers. She pushed her chair forward.

"What's it *like*, dying?" she said. "Joanne Solarski from the pharmacy ran to the house and told me you were dead. Everyone said so. But you're alive – you came back. So tell me, what happens? Are the stories right? Did you see an angel, Jim? Did you move toward the light? Tell me."

I'd never heard her talk like this. Mostly it was *Don't bother me now*, or *Has anyone seen my teeth?* Here she was, sounding really interested.

"I didn't die," I said.

"*Something* happened to you," she insisted. "You're different, Jim. Saying you were glad to see me, just now.

That didn't sound like you at all. And you've been smiling. There – you're doing it now. You didn't used to smile this much. Were you touched by an angel?"

"I don't think so."

"I saw a TV show about a soul who couldn't rest until she showed the cops where the missing child was. Do you have a mission like that, Jim? Someone to save?"

"I don't know."

"I bet you do. Who's Marcie?" Peering at me.

"Marcie?"

"You're smiling again. She's someone, isn't she? Marcie. You called that name out when you were sleeping."

I tried to think back, but I was missing a connection. Wires in my brain hanging loose.

"It was probably a dream," I said.

She stood up, checking her purse for cigarettes. "Well, I got to go. You look weird with no hair, Jim. Like a ghost, you know? Like you're not here. That's what Cassie thinks. She won't visit, because she doesn't think you are really you."

"What?"

"I told her you were in the hospital, but she won't believe me. She is sure you're dead."

My crazy sister.

"Well, bye, Jim."

"Bye, Ma." I struggled to my feet. Stood awkwardly beside my bed. "Thanks for coming by."

"There you go, saying thanks. Something happened to you, Jim. You're not the kid I used to know."

CHAPTER 19

As the days went by I continued to act strange for me. Like saying thank you to the lady with the train-whistle breath who brought me my meals. I'd open my mouth to make fun of her, and then I'd catch myself and say thank you instead. Or like when Chester dropped his cane on the way to the bathroom and slowly toppled, like a tree cut down by a lumberjack. I was going to laugh, but instead I hurried over to help him. That seemed like the right thing to do, and yet it didn't fit the me I remembered.

Or when I found my mean nurse crying, and I was sympathetic. We were outside, me with a smoke I'd borrowed from Chester's pack and her with her cell phone. She was sitting by herself on a low stone wall, staring down at a text message, sniffing and swallowing. I went over and sat beside her on the wall and put my hand on her shoulder.

She snapped the phone shut and took off her glasses to wipe her eyes. And I patted her shoulder and said, "There there."

I am not kidding. *There there*, like I was her dad or something.

She didn't tell me to put out my cigarette. She sniffed and said I was a good kid. And that men were shits.

"You're right about that," I said.

Turned out she was upset because her boyfriend had just dumped her. "I should have known when he called me *Zelda baby* last week. Zelda baby! He tried to cover it up, saying he thought he was phoning his sister, and her name is Zelda. But he doesn't have a sister. He's stupid."

"I'll say."

She patted me on the cheek. Her hand felt soft. With her hair a bit messed up, and her glasses off, she looked okay. "What's your name if it's not Zelda?" I asked.

Bertha, she told me.

"Bertha." I was going to say that's a nice name, except it isn't. I mean, it really isn't. I didn't know what to say next, but it didn't matter because I let out this giant fart. Hospitals are big on bran muffins and stuff like that, and . . . well, there was no smooth way to pretend it didn't happen. The fart ripped the air apart and then rumbled on and on, like a long thunderclap. We froze, both of us, like statues, and there was just the noise and gas.

And we laughed and laughed. Bertha was crying, she was laughing so hard. I felt awkward, but sort of pleased, you know, for taking her mind off her troubles.

I was not used to feeling like this.

Bertha fanned the air. "And I thought your cigarette smelled bad," she said, still laughing. "You'd better go back inside, Jim."

I had a visitor that afternoon during the soap opera. Chester was in his bed, and I was in the chair with my feet up. We had the TV angled so we could both see it. We'd been watching *Life After Life* all week. Chester was really into it.

The knock came near the end of the episode. I turned. A woman in a kerchief and sunglasses stood in the doorway.

"I'm looking for Jim, the young man who was run over," she said.

"That's me."

She hesitated. "I don't want to interrupt."

"Come on in, ma'am," said Chester. "Sit on Jim's bed there and watch the end of the show with us."

"Really?"

I lifted my feet off the bed. She took a step forward. "Well, if you're sure."

She took off her glasses and sat neatly, her plastic shopping bag in her lap. She watched with a frown on her face, like she was studying the soap opera in film school.

INT. OFFICE BUILDING – NIGHT.

RAVEN WORMCAST (32), a dangerous beauty, is moving through a darkened office with the aid of a flashlight. She is dressed in black turtleneck and jeans. She opens a filing cabinet and flips through the files until she comes to one marked BRICK McCOY.

RAVEN (mutters)

Oh, Brick. You poor, innocent fool!

Now where oh where is that alibi of yours . . .

She opens the file, finds a paper marked AFFIDAVIT, and reads . . .

> RAVEN
> Aha!

She removes the affidavit, replaces the folder in the
filing cabinet. She crosses to the shredder, turns it on,
and feeds in the affidavit.
> . RAVEN (gloats)
> Now you have no defense, Brick. They'll find
> you guilty. If only your sister could testify . . .
> But she can't! She can't!!

RAVEN laughs maniacally. Cut to –

INT. BEDROOM – NIGHT.
TINTORETTA McCOY (26) slumps in a wheelchair.
Her face is beautiful, her body completely paralyzed.
She is alone in her room. Tears trickle down her face.
ROLL CREDITS.

"That Raven is something else," said Chester.
"What a hellcat!"

"Sure is," I said.

"What'll Brick do for an alibi now?"

"Don't know."

"The girl in the wheelchair is Brick's sister," he
explained to the lady in the kerchief. "Her name's
Tintoretta. She could give him an alibi for the time of the
murder, but her evidence might not be alleged in court
because she can't talk."

"Allowed," I said.

"Huh?"

"You said alleged. You mean allowed. Her evidence might not be allowed in court."

"Oh, yeah. She talks by blinking her eyes, ma'am. One blink for yes, and two for no. Like this would be: no."

He blinked twice.

"I see," said the woman.

"Alleged, eh?" said Chester with a sidelong glance at me. "Jim here is awful sharp. I have trouble keeping up with him."

He struggled up from the bed and said he was heading outside for a smoke. Normally he'd have a nap now, but he was giving me some privacy. He was okay, Chester.

I stayed in my chair. The lady got to her feet, faced me.

"I came to say I'm sorry, Jim," she said. "I'm the one who ran you over on Tuesday. Do you remember?"

I shook my head.

"Oh." She sniffed. "Oh, dear. Well, it was my fault, and I wanted to apologize. I'm not normally an aggressive driver, but I was upset, and I didn't look where I was going. As a matter of fact, I was on my way to the hospital. Not this one – St. Joe's, in the west end. My daughter, Marcie, was dying."

Something was tugging at my memory now, like a dog worrying at the blanket, trying to pull it off you. "Marcie?" I said.

"I took her in with a bad fever, and they kept her overnight. I went home in the morning to change, and they called me to say she'd fallen and was unconscious. When I ran you over I was hysterical. I was afraid I'd killed you and that my daughter would die before I got to see her."

She twisted the plastic handles of the shopping bag, remembering.

"Marcie got better, but I was still worried about you. I've been calling the hospital every few days. When they told me you were out of danger, it was like I got my life back too. I wanted to see you and say I was sorry."

She opened the bag on the table next to my bed. Inside were grapes, black, firm, and round.

"Marcie loves grapes," she said. "I thought you might too."

I had a good feeling about this lady. It's like when a song starts on the radio. You don't recognize it from the intro, but you know you like it.

"Can you forgive me, Jim?" she said.

My head and hand and body hurt, I had a hole in my throat, and I couldn't remember the past three days. But I had this feeling about her.

"Sure," I said.

CHAPTER 20

L ate that night I woke up with Bertha standing beside my bed.

"Are you all right, Jim?" she whispered. "You were moaning."

"Uh," I said.

I'd been dreaming of a dark-eyed girl who fed me grapes and offered to show me her underpants if I could say her name. Only I couldn't think of her name. Now I was awake, with a tent pole between my legs. I was lying on my back and the sheet was the tent, if you know what I mean. I was embarrassed. My dick wasn't, though. It moved on its own under the sheet, like it was saying, *Ta-da!*

"I'm glad you're awake, Jim," she said. "It gives me a chance to say good-bye. I'm changing my rotation. Starting tomorrow I'll be upstairs in the neonatal unit. You'll be going home soon, and I won't see you again. I'm going to miss you."

We shook hands. Her palm felt soft and smooth. So soft.

Ta-da! said my dick.

I closed my eyes in embarrassment . . . and found myself thinking about the kerchief lady's daughter. The girl who'd had the fever. She'd been the one in my dream! She had striped underpants. And she loved grapes. And she'd kissed me. How did I know these things about her?

Somehow, that's how. I didn't understand, but I knew they were true.

"Marcie," I said.

"*What?*"

I opened my eyes. I was still holding the nurse's hand.

"It's Bertha." She jerked her hand away. "My name is Bertha."

"I know," I said. "I was thinking of someone else."

She folded her arms across the front of her uniform.

"Oh, Jim! You're just like all the rest of them. You're talking to one girl and thinking of another one."

She turned to go.

"Wait, Bertha," I said.

"Don't *Bertha* me!"

She yanked open my privacy curtain on her way out so that light streamed in from the corridor.

Ta-da! said my dick. Stupid thing had no sense of timing. I shifted under the covers, turning awkwardly onto my side.

Another dream came later that night – not a good one. I was staring out a window into the dark. Something scary was approaching from behind. I couldn't move, not even to turn and face it. The thing came closer and closer. I could feel its moist breath on the back of my neck. Whatever it was gave a strange, soft, mewing cry. I forced my head far enough around to see two eyes glowing in the dark. Then all of a sudden I was running, and the eyes were following me. They turned into car headlights. I fell, and the headlights were on top of me. I woke up gasping.

I had twisted the covers round my feet. Straightening them out, I saw movement. What was it? I leaned over the bed but couldn't make anything out. There was a faint smell I hadn't noticed before. Not a hospital smell. This was more like home: rotting food, sweat, fear. Yeck.

I shivered and remembered a phrase of my ma's. She'd be sitting in the kitchen with a drink and a smoke, and a sudden shudder would pass over her, like wind on grass.

"Someone just walked over my grave," she'd say.

CHAPTER 21

I stayed in hospital another week. Dr. Driver came by with her tape recorder again, but I couldn't tell her much more about the accident. I remembered chasing Lloyd, but not why. She asked if Lloyd was a friend of mine. I said no. I asked her when my memory would come back. She told me not to get too frustrated. I'm not frustrated, I told her – just forgetful.

All this time I was noticing that Chester was going downhill. I mean, we're all going downhill all the time, but that week Chester put on some serious speed. By Friday, he couldn't do anything without gasping for breath, his mouth hanging open like a dog's on a hot day. Our nurse (a new one named Sam, with braces and squeaky shoes) gave him a breathing kit and a wheelchair and took away all the cigarettes.

"One of those packs is mine," I lied. I knew Chester would want to have an emergency supply.

"You're too young to smoke," Sam told me, pocketing them and squeaking off to the nursing station.

"Thanks . . . for trying," Chester wheezed. Talking was hard work for him.

I put a finger to my lips. Reaching under my mattress, I pulled out a battered pack. He laughed long enough to worry me.

"You're . . . holding," he whispered, when he was through coughing.

"Yeah."

A couple of hours later he rolled his chair over to my bed.

"Jim."

"What?"

He dropped his eyes to my mattress.

"You want to go to the smoking lounge?" I said. I was talking about the bathroom down the hall. It was our usual place.

He nodded.

"You sure?"

"Please, Jim."

I figured he was old enough to decide if he wanted a smoke. And I didn't want him to beg anymore. I pushed him down the hall. His wheelchair had a basket at the back for his air tank and a pole for his drip. He didn't talk. He was too busy breathing.

Not a big room, the bathroom. He sat in his chair, I got the toilet seat. "Careful," he said, pointing to his air tank. "This is oxygen. Burns . . . like gasoline."

He always said that.

I waited for him to turn it off, then lit up for both of us.

"I'm glad you don't tell me I'm stupid," he said. "I know I'm stupid. I'm eighty-three, and I been smoking since I was your age. That's . . . a long time. They say I don't stop, it's gonna kill me. I say I'm almost dead now. What are they saving me? A month? A week?"

It took him a long time to get this out.

"A day?" He took a drag, coughed.

"Come on, Chester, you'll make it. When I was in my coma, I was almost dead. And I came back."

"Yeah, but you're a kid. You're not supposed to die. Me, I'm due. When that angel taps me on the shoulder, I ain't fighting."

That afternoon Dr. Driver came to give me a last look over before letting me go home. She checked my eyes, the back of my head, and my fingertips. Her hair was in its usual ponytail. Her skin smelled clean.

I was trying to watch our soap opera, but the doctor kept interrupting. Friday is a key day for a soap, got to set the story up for the weekend. Yesterday the judge had decided to admit Tintoretta's evidence to support her brother Brick's alibi. Today we were in court.

"Pay attention, Jim." Dr. Driver grabbed my chin, turned my head to face her. "You're not better yet," she said. "We cleared up the bleeding in your skull, and you've been stable for more than a week, but it's still delicate in there. I want you to take it easy when you get home. Lots of rest. No strenuous exercise. I'm going to give you some pills. They make the blood thinner, so you're less likely to have a seizure."

I'd been sneaking glances at the TV over her shoulder, but I came back to her then.

"Seizure?" I said. "Like I'll spaz out? Start rolling on the floor?"

"You hurt the back of your head, Jim. That's the vision center of the brain. I want you to pay careful attention to your eyes when you get home. If you start seeing strange things – flashing light, for instance – go to the hospital at once."

She gave me a school notebook with a spiral binding. "This is for you. It's a memory book. Bits and pieces about the accident should start coming back to you soon. I want you to write them in the book. Any memory you get – a flash, a picture, a feeling – put it down. It'll help you."

I took the notebook.

"I don't think anyone's ever given me one of these before," I said.

She reached into an inside pocket in her white coat. "Can you promise to take your pills, Jim? Take one every day. I should give them to your mom, but I figure you'll be looking after yourself. These are free samples. Do not sell them – they're no good to anyone but you. When you run out of pills, come back and I'll give you more. Make sure –"

She broke off. Chester was propped up in his bed to watch the TV, but his head had fallen off to one side and he was gagging. His skin was the color of a cloudy sky. He fumbled at the breathing hose, like he was trying to pull it out.

"Nurse!" The doc leaped over my bed, ran to Chester. "Nurse!"

She pulled the privacy curtain so that I couldn't see Chester's side of the room anymore.

Sam the nurse hurried in pushing a cart. After her came a tall doctor who didn't seem to be in much of a hurry. He stopped to glare at me before gliding behind the curtain.

I felt something heavy inside me. The feeling wasn't about me, though. It was about Chester and this quiet doc dressed in gray. I didn't like the heavy feeling. I went back to the soap opera.

Tintoretta's eyes filled the TV screen. Her pupils were like dark caves, surrounded by a forest of eyelashes. The court reporter was counting eye blinks – one for yes and two for no. The defense lawyer asked, *Were you with your brother on the night in question?* This was the key question because it proved the alibi. The court reporter leaned toward Tintoretta to make sure. Only, he'd eaten a hamburger with extra onions for lunch, and his breath was strong enough to make Tintoretta's eyes water, so she blinked twice when she meant to blink once.

Two blinks, said the court reporter. *The answer to the question is, No.*

The courtroom erupted. Raven gesticulated in triumph. Brick protested and was dragged away. The judge pounded her gavel. The final shot was a close-up – Tintoretta with her eyes shut tight. We cut to a commercial about disinfectant.

Chester raced out from behind the privacy curtain with a pink-lipped grin on his face, looking years younger. Decades, maybe. No wheelchair, no breathing tube or IV. Nothing. He waved vigorously at me, excited as hell, like a little kid getting out of school.

My heart jumped, I was so relieved. "Hey, Chester!" I called out.

He kept smiling, and I realized he was dead.

"Oh, crap," I said.

He didn't seem to mind being dead, though. He came right over to my chair and gave me a hug. I didn't feel it, but that's what he was doing. He stood in front of me with his arms outspread, taking a deep breath. Like he was showing me what he could do now, that he couldn't do when he was alive.

"Yeah yeah," I said. "But are you happy?"

He bent down so that his eyes were level with mine. And he blinked once, hard. Him and Tintoretta.

And he vanished like that.

I started to sob. Chester might have been better off dead than alive, but I couldn't stop the tears. The harder I cried, the more I remembered. Chester's ghost joined all the other ghosts I had seen on the street and in that awful hotel in the sky. I kept crying. It was like there were walls in my mind between my accident and waking up, and my tears were a flood, washing away the walls, so that I remembered everything that had happened to me since I got run over by Marcie's mom, what I'd seen and learned and almost lost. Why did the knowledge come then? I don't know. Maybe crying had something to do with it. Maybe it matters that you can cry for someone who isn't you.

They brought out the body on a gurney, Dr. Driver and Sam and the quiet doctor who'd glared at me.

I remembered *his* name now. He was a ghost too – a Slayer. That's why he was gray and didn't talk. He looked angrier than usual, and I knew why. Chester wasn't going to the Jordan Arms. He was gone, free of the earth – and Morgan was still stuck here, as he had been for three hundred years.

Chester being free made me want to smile even though I was still crying. Morgan glowered at me. Which reminded me of how he'd failed with me. I was free too. I had my whole life ahead of me to live well in. Morgan looked so funny I started to laugh, which was a mistake because the tears and laughter got confused and I had to cough.

Dr. Driver came over. "I have some bad news, Jim," she said. "I'm afraid that your friend Chester is –"

"I know," I said, catching my breath. "I know."

Morgan shook a fist at me and drifted out the door. The bullet holes in the back of his shirt looked like cigarette burns.

Ma came for me during afternoon snack time. I gave her a hug.

"What's that for?"

"I'm glad to see you, Ma," I said. "I can't *wait* to go home!"

"Huh."

The hospital staff didn't know about Chester dying, so the lady with the train-whistle breath brought him a bran muffin. I thanked her and ate his along with mine.

CHAPTER 22

When I got home, everything was the same. Mold on the wallpaper, dirty dishes in the kitchen, rumpled sheets on my bed. Hot wind moving the curtains on my window, horns honking on Roncesvalles, TV playing downstairs.

Everything was the same, except me. I was thinner from hospital food, and softer from no exercise, and almost bald. I had a scar on the front of my neck, and pills to take. And a mission.

The morning after I got home, I put on shorts and sandals and a T-shirt with a picture of Bob Marley on it. Dressed to redeem. I took a twenty-dollar bill from my stash, crossed Roncy to the K Fruit Store, and bought a fifty-cent plum. The old Korean guy took my bill and made change.

I waved it away. "Keep it," I said. The twenty was an installment. My plan was to gradually pay him back for all the fruit I had stolen over the past year or so.

He frowned. "Your change," he said.

"I don't want it," I said.

I bit into the plum. "Good plums," I said. "Thank you very much." When I turned to go, he ran after me.

"Change," he said, holding out the money.

"No, no," I said. "No change."

"Please take," he said. "Please!"

He sounded desperate.

"Do you know who I am?" I said. "I'm the kid who steals fruit and laughs at you."

He shook his head. "No."

"Yes! I was in an accident a couple of weeks ago. You saw me. You called me the no good one who robs your place of business. Remember? Ambulance?" He frowned. If only I spoke Korean. "You know, *ambulance*," I said.

I made a siren noise. *Eeee-awwww-eeeee-awwww*.

He frowned.

I tried it again. Sounded more like a donkey than an ambulance. We were on the sidewalk in front of his store, standing next to a display of peaches. A mom with a stroller stopped to stare at me. I felt embarrassed.

Mr. K pulled a plastic bag from a nearby roll, put my change in the bag, and tied it up with neat, sure motions from his spider fingers.

"Clean," he said, holding out the bag.

Did he think I was afraid of his dirty hands? "No, no," I said. "That's not it."

"You take!" he said, angrily now, putting the plastic bag on top of the plums and going back into the store.

Drat. It wasn't easy, apologizing. The lady pushed her stroller away, chatting down into it. Probably telling her kid not to grow up to be a crazy teenager.

I took the money and tried to jog to Raf's place. I only got about halfway there before I had to stop. My legs felt like they were made of Plasticine. I was in worse shape than I thought. Raf lived with his dad in a basement apartment on Westminster. No one answered my knock. I found a stone and scratched a *J* on the wall beside the basement door, low down where his dad wouldn't look. Raf knew that meant to call me.

I walked home down Roncy, thinking to stop in at Jerry's and see whether Raf was there, but the place was closed. I went home.

Muggier inside than out. Ma and Cassie were watching a soap opera (not *Life After Life*. You know, I never did find out what happened to Brick and Raven. Without Chester, the show wasn't interesting) while the fan blew hot air around the living room. My sister turned her head away from me, shuddering.

I had to remember to have a talk with Cassie.

"Where were you, Jim?" asked Ma.

"Out."

"Well," she said and went back to the TV. Like she was going to ask me something and then forgot.

I went upstairs and had a nap.

Next day was a beauty – sunny, dry, clean. The very best kind of summer day. I walked down Roncy to the Goodwill store and paid two dollars for a shirt I didn't want. I dumped the shirt in the donations bin outside the store and walked home feeling okay. I thought about doing that for the fruit store – buying a plum and then putting it back on my way out – but I figured it would take me too long to make good all I'd stolen.

On the way home I turned down Galley Avenue. I walked east to Sorauren, then checked back through the maze of laneways running between Galley and Pearson.

I was looking for a blue Pontiac with a cracked windshield. No luck.

I walked up to Jerry's, but the place was closed. I stood on the corner, wondering what there was at home to drink, when Maq bumped into me. His eyes were half closed and he was bobbing his head to whatever music he was listening to. He stopped. "Sorry," he said with a quick smile. "Wasn't looking where I was going."

We hadn't spoken in years, but I recognized him at once. And he was on my list. What a piece of luck.

"No, Maq," I said, blocking his path. "*I'm* sorry."

He wore a colorful shirt and tight jeans, carried a bag from the grocery store. The warm breeze ruffled his mop of red hair into a blaze. He squinted at me, pulled a wire out of his ear.

"What was that?"

"Sorry," I said again.

"For what?"

I wondered how to tackle a delicate topic after a gap of years and decided to simply push ahead.

"For picking a fight with you. Beating you up. For, well . . . for tearing your arm off."

I could hear the music he was listening to, faint and tinny, through the end of the headphone. Familiar music.

"Who are you?" he asked. When I told him, his face cleared partway. He remembered who I was, but he wasn't pleased about it.

"Jim," he said. "Big, bad Jim. It's been a long time, hasn't it. How you doing, anyway?"

I'm good, I told him.

"Really?"

"Yeah. Real good."

He nodded slowly. "Yeah, maybe. Maybe you are."

I could see why he'd have doubts about me. I didn't blame him. "Anyway," I said, "I wanted to let you know I feel bad about beating you up when we were kids. That's all."

"You didn't beat me up."

"Well . . . pulling off your arm, then."

"Forget about that. It used to happen all the time. And, uh, thanks, Jim. You know, you do seem different. Saying sorry – you didn't have to do that. Not after all this time."

He had the grocery bag on his fake arm, I saw. The hand looked much more real than I remembered. The fingers could close and everything.

I could have walked on now, but I didn't want to. He didn't seem to want to either. "So, your arm used to come off a lot?"

"Oh yeah. My papa did it himself once on the Ferris wheel, pulling me back when I wanted to look over the edge of the chair."

"What?"

"Yeah, he's afraid of heights and jerked my arm too hard. Then he panicked and dropped it. It fell right beside the carney who was running the Ferris wheel. He screamed, and, well, it was all pretty embarrassing."

I laughed and caught myself.

"Sorry," I said.

"That's okay. It's funny now."

He still had one headphone in his ear. I asked him about the music he was listening to. His face brightened.

"It's Schubert," he said. "You like Schubert, Jim?"

I told him I liked the bit I could hear.

"It's from a Bugs Bunny cartoon, right?"

He gave me headphones, put the song back to the beginning, and made me listen to the whole thing. Funny picture, eh? Two teenagers standing close together on the sidewalk on a sunny afternoon, headphone wires leading from my ears to his knapsack, me listening first to the music (*Deedly deeedly*, remember?) and then to the story he told me of a father, his doomed child, and the magical Erl King who takes the boy's life. Cool, I said. And it was.

He took back his headphones but didn't put them back in.

"Say, Jim. I've got some lemonade mix here. Why don't you come to my place and have a glass? It's not far. Just down the street, beside the public school. Come on."

CHAPTER 23

Maq's place smelled of paint, soap, and food. Nice smells.

"Papa, I brought a friend home!" he called from the front hall. The word made me feel funny. He led me to the kitchen, a small room with two windows side by side. No, on closer inspection one of them was a painting. But, you know, it looked *exactly* like the real thing. Same size and shape, same color of the what-do-you-call-it, the wood around the glass. Same bumps on the glass. Same view of the brick wall on the house next door.

"That is so cool," I said.

"It's a trick. What the French call a *trompe l'oeil*. It means the eye is fooled. My dad painted it."

"Your dad is an amazing artist."

There was a chuckle from the doorway.

"I like this friend of yours!" cried Maq's dad. "I like him a lot!"

"This is Jim, Papa."

"*Allo*, Jim." He gave me a sweeping wave. He was still a big guy with a big nose, and his accent was as thick as it had been all those years ago when he'd carried Maq inside with the plastic arm dangling. He was someone you couldn't help noticing – bigger, louder, more boisterous than anyone around. He was like a large dog in a small room.

"Jim." He grinned. "A smart boy. A bright boy. He knows I am an amazing artist."

Maq mixed the lemonade, added ice cubes, and poured. I watched carefully. He handed me my glass and smiled. "My new prosthesis," he said, making a fist. "Just got it last month. Want me to take it off and show you?"

"No." Quickly.

His papa stared at me, like he was looking underneath my skin, trying to see what I was made of. "Do you study art, Jim?"

"Uh, no."

"But you understand it."

"I do?" I must have made a funny face because he burst out laughing. That's a common expression, but Maq's dad came close to doing it. He practically exploded into laughter.

"You like my window, hey? Well, then, you understand art. You know what the artist does. He paints the soul. He paints illusion and desire, life and death and afterlife. That is what an artist does."

He drank his lemonade in one long swig and sighed deeply.

"You know things, Jim," he said. "Your face has depth in it. You see what others do not."

I drank.

"I have reason, yes? You understand what I am talking about."

He had large yellow eyes, I noticed. Like a lion. He was totally serious.

"Yes," I said. "I know things."

"*Bon*, I will show you my portrait of Maq's mother, my dead wife."

I turned to Maq. He shrugged.

His dad handed the empty glass back to his son. "This poor boy never knew his mama. But me, I remember her well. I feel her presence very near. Do you know what it's like to feel a presence you cannot see?"

He led me to a big open room that was so bright it hummed. You couldn't see where the light was coming from – skylights were frosted over and lightbulbs were hidden up in the ceiling – but the place was as bright as an operating room. And yet the light wasn't harsh. I didn't want to squint. I felt I could see better in that room. Pictures were stacked on the floor along the walls like the junk in Jerry's store. The only piece of furniture was a table, covered in colored tubes and coffee cups. The smell of paint was very strong.

The light seemed to concentrate, gather up its energy, and fling itself at the far wall. On that wall, hung at eye level, was a picture the size of my bedroom door.

The fake window got to me because it looked so real, so true to life. This picture wasn't like that. Maq's dad hadn't tried to make his wife look lifelike. Her face was all straight lines and way too big for her body. One of her arms came out at a funny angle, fingers splayed. She was supposed to be lying down on a couch, but the way she was painted she looked like she was floating over it, her hospital gown drooping. But she was real too. Her expression was sad, needy, intense. That was exactly how she looked. I recognized her right away. It was a picture of Denise, my Mourner. She was Maq's mom.

His dad was watching me. I don't know what my face told him, but he nodded as if he was satisfied. Then he brought out a handkerchief the size of a surrender flag and blew his nose.

Sunlight slanted down onto the porch, making me squint. Maq sat in a swing chair. His papa stood with a heavy arm around my shoulder, talking hard. "It is fourteen years that Denise died. But I am always feeling her presence nearby. Sometimes it is like she is in the room with me. You know that feeling – being watched?" he asked me.

I nodded.

"So I paint this picture for me, and for Maq who never knew his mother. And for her too. For her presence. Do you understand?"

I didn't say anything. His dad squeezed my shoulder hard. "You saw something in the picture, didn't you? She spoke to you, my wife."

I nodded.

"Pictures do that, when you know how to look at them. You have the eyes of a painter, Jim. You can see the real window, and the fake. Eh? Tell me, what did she say to you, my Denise?"

"Well, she misses *you* terribly." I caught Maq's eye. "And she loves you more than anything in the world."

Maq didn't say anything for a second. His throat slid up and down. He was swallowing. Maybe it was a lot to swallow.

"And the picture?" asked his father. "What of that?"

"It's a masterpiece."

His smile returned like springtime.

"Yes, it is."

CHAPTER 24

Next morning I got up before anyone else in the house. The kitchen clock said 8:45. I could almost have been on time for school, if there was any school. A hot day already. Rumble of distant thunder. Made me smile to think how much Cassie was going to complain about it. I didn't mind the heat. I took a deep breath of it, heading out the door.

I still must have been smiling when I got to Roncy because a baba – black kerchief, sweater, cane – grinned up at me. Two teeth in her mouth, both as yellow as corn. She said something in Polish.

"You bet," I said.

A lazy hornet buzzed around the plum display at the K Fruit Store this morning. I watched it for a sec. Hornets are cool but kind of scary. They seem so laid-back and droopy, barely enough energy to fly around, and then they go crazy and start stinging you. I picked a nectarine from the top of a neat pyramid and went to the back of the store to pay. Mr. K was not in charge of the cash register today. A kid – maybe his son or nephew – sat behind the cash register, reading a comic book in Korean.

This was my chance. I held out all the money in my pocket and told him I didn't want any change.

He frowned. "Why not?"

"The guy who runs this store lent me some money yesterday," I said. "I told him I'd pay it back. You just put this . . . thirty-seven dollars in the till and call it square."

Kid was my age. He put down the comic and stared at me through his wire-rimmed glasses "You talking about *Harabujee?*" he said. At least that's what the word sounded like. "My *grandfather* gave you money?"

"I dunno," I said. "Skinny old guy who's always here."

"Yeah that's *Harabujee.* But I don't get it. He's always talking about how hard he works. And how lazy everyone else is. Hell, he doesn't pay me. There's no way he'd just give you money."

The hornet drifted back. Or maybe it was another hornet. Anyway, it was buzzing in lazy circles around my head. I felt the situation getting out of control. I pushed the cash at the kid. "Take it," I said.

"If *Harabujee* gave you that money, you still have to pay for the nectarine."

"Forget the nectarine. I'll put it back. Take the cash, okay?"

"Just let me check." He turned his head and shouted something over his shoulder, into the room at the back of the store.

The hornet was hovering near me. I took a step back.

"Don't bother to check," I said. "How about if I –"

Mr. K showed up, wiping his mouth. He smiled politely at me and then said something quick and sharp in Korean. His grandson started to explain, but Mr. K shook his head after three seconds. THAT IS RIDICULOUS! he said. (I don't *know* if he said that, but that's sure what it sounded like.)

"That's what I thought, *Harabujee*," said the kid. "Which is why I –"

Mr. K interrupted, talking faster and faster. And getting angry. Not at me, though – at his grandson. He talked right over the kid's explanations.

"But I *wasn't* overcharging him, *Harabujee*," he said. "He wanted to . . . He . . . He offered . . ."

Mr. K never even stopped to breathe.

I tried to say something, but they both ignored me.

The hornet landed on the top of the cash register and sat there, stretching its wings gently.

Mr. K had the comic book in his hand now, shaking it in the kid's face.

"Yes, *Harabujee*," he said. He had his head down now. He'd given up. "I know I shouldn't be reading this."

I turned and walked out, carefully replacing the nectarine on the top of the pyramid. More hornets were buzzing around. One of the plums had burst, I noticed, and the insects were enjoying the flesh and juice. The cash went back into my pocket. Mr. K's voice rose behind me like a bird in flight.

I walked down to Galley Avenue. This time I went west, checking laneways and on-street parking on the south side. No blue Pontiacs, no slender teenaged girls. But when I got back to Roncy I caught sight of a familiar figure a block down, waiting at the streetcar stop. Something about the way this kid held himself, leaning forward and a bit hesitant. Was it Lloyd? His hair was the right ginger color. I was about to call out, but a streetcar arrived and he got on. That was that.

I was hungry. I'd eaten some puffed wheat at home, but we'd run out of sugar, and without sugar puffed wheat is not really breakfast. It is barely cereal. And I still had thirty-seven dollars in my pocket. One good thing about Roncy is that you are never far from a donut shop. Crossing the street, I looked both ways. I was paying for my double-double and honey cruller when someone hit me from behind. It was Sparks, alone. I was surprised. I've seen Cap without him, but not the other way round.

"You Jim?" He wore a sleeveless shirt to show his cantaloupe biceps.

"Me Jim," I said, like Tarzan. "You Sparks."

He didn't get it. He frowned, his one eyebrow bending in the middle.

"You sure? You sound like Jim, but you don't look like him."

Sparks is not the quickest cockroach in the race.

"Yeah, I'm sure. I know who I am."

"Cap wants to see you." Doubtfully. "If you're really Jim."

"Great," I said. "I've been looking for Cap too." Raf hadn't called, which meant that he hadn't been home to see the sign by his door. Cap would know where he was. "What's going on at Jerry's? How come the store is closed?"

Sparks frowned.

"You come with me. Okay?"

"'Kay."

"We'll see Cap."

"Got it."

No point in discussing things with Sparks. He wouldn't understand. He'd do what he was told – bring me to Cap if he saw me. And anyway he was the size of a small building. He could have carried me over his shoulder like a baby.

CHAPTER 25

The sun was surrounded by clouds that looked like dumplings – they even seemed heavy, like they would weigh on your stomach if you ate them. We walked up Roncy and down Geoffrey, Sparks at my elbow. Moms with strollers and off-shift workers with cigarettes and shopping bags stayed out of our way. I kept my head down, in case I ran into Marcie. If you're asking was I ashamed of being seen with Sparks, the answer is yes. I didn't want the first girl I'd ever kissed to know the old piece-of-crap side of me.

We didn't see her.

Cap lived on Sorauren, in an old factory that had been divided into units. His place was on the second floor, a huge triangle-shaped room. TV room, kitchen, bedroom in the three corners, with enough empty floor space in the middle to play tennis. Kind of cool. Sparks let himself in. Cap was on the couch watching a Nas video. Sparks handed him a coffee and a chocolate donut and kept another for himself.

"This guy here is Jim," he said. "I think."

"So he is," said Cap. "You look horrible, Jim. Like a cancer kid."

He turned down the sound. The video kept playing in the background. I stood in front of him, smiling to show I knew it was a joke. Cancer is hilarious, all right.

"But you're back, and that's the main thing. I saw you get run over, you know." Cap took a sip of coffee, grimaced. "I was on the street with Sparks here when you went under that car. I was like, Gee that's too bad about Jim. We were upset, weren't we, Sparks?"

Sparks and I didn't say anything. We knew Cap was lying.

"Anyway, I'm glad you're here now. I want to talk to you about our friend Rafal. Your partner."

Cap took a delicate bite of donut. The video played in the background, Nas and The Game trading lines. I stayed silent. Cap was going to tell me what I wanted to know.

"Raf's in jail," said Cap. "Arrested on the scene, and they still haven't let him out. Pineview Youth Detention Center, out in Etobicoke. I talked to his lawyer about the charges. Raf's still a minor, and joyriding is a misdemeanor. You wouldn't think there'd be a problem."

Cap gestured for me to come closer. I leaned down and he spoke right near my ear. "But the cops aren't talking about joyriding. This is Raf's second arrest. The cops figure he's part of a major car-theft ring. The lawyer's worried for me."

"Why's Raf's lawyer worried for *you*?"

Cap drank coffee. "Because I'm paying him. He's my lawyer."

"But you're not in jail."

"Not yet I'm not. And I don't want to go. Neither does Jerry. That's why he's in the Bahamas now." Cap poked a finger at me. "What about you, Jim? You were at the scene.

They'll have your fingerprints. D'you want to go to jail?"

"No."

"'Course you don't. You're a smart guy. So here's what you do. You go to Pineview to visit Raf, and you tell him not to say anything, no matter what the cops promise him. Can you do that?"

Cap handed his empty coffee cup to Sparks.

"See, Jim, the cops really want the car thieves. They might offer Raf a deal. They might tell him he'll go free if he says who he's working for. I don't want that. I do not want my name showing up on police files. I do not want any talk about me or Jerry. Do you understand?"

Sparks gave a small squeak, like a mouse asking for a piece of cheese.

"Or Sparks. Or any of us here." Cap gave me a smile so creepy I wanted to give it back without opening it. "We're a family, and family don't sell each other to the cops. Right, Jim?"

The video was over. Nas showed his scarred back to the camera.

"I'll talk to Raf," I said.

"Good boy."

I took a deep breath. "But I want to make something clear, Cap. I'm out."

"Out? Out of what?"

"The gang. Whatever we are at Jerry's. You and Sparks and the guys in the garage. I'll tell Raf what you said about talking to the cops. I'll do that for you. But nothing else. I won't be coming round Jerry's store. You don't have to worry about me asking questions anymore. I don't want to know anything. I don't want to work for you ever again."

I still had a half-full coffee cup in my hand. It was cold by now.

"I nearly died last week, Cap," I said. "I know things I didn't used to. I know what pieces of crap we are. And all that stuff about us being family – I know that's crap too. I saw you and Sparks laughing while I was lying in the middle of the road. Don't ask me how, but I did. You didn't care about me, and you don't care about Raf. All you care about is you. Well, screw you, Cap. And –"

"Watch out!"

I knew that voice. I ducked as soon as I heard it. Sparks's punch went over my head.

CHAPTER 26

H e swung so hard that he lost his balance, stumbling past me and ending up on his knees.

"And screw you too, Sparks," I said.

Cap swore quietly. My coffee cup had ended up in his lap. He stood up, holding his pants away from his skin.

"Leave him alone," he said to Sparks, who was back on his feet with his fist cocked.

I was safe enough for now. They still needed me to talk to Raf. What I wanted was to stay safe afterwards. And I had an idea about that. Instead of leaving, I lifted my head and spoke to the ghost in the three-piece suit.

"Thanks, Tadeusz."

An expression of surprise broke across his face. He wasn't used to being thanked.

"So this is what you Mourners do – you warn people of danger. And you can show up anywhere, anytime."

He nodded.

"'Cause I remember once when I was getting off the streetcar late at night, I thought I heard someone tell me to watch out, and I stopped on the bottom step, and this pickup truck came roaring past. Would have run me over if I'd kept going. I looked around, but I was alone on the streetcar. So that was you, or Denise maybe. Or some other Mourner."

He nodded again. Sad little smile on his face.

"Well, all I can say is that your timing is real good."

Sparks and Cap seemed puzzled. I must have looked crazy, talking to the air.

"Who's there, Jim?" said Cap. "Who you talking to?"

"Tadeusz Kosinski."

Cap went very still.

"You remember Tadeusz, don't you, Cap? Used to live around here. Fat guy, always dressed nice. Used to kick people out of their homes. A couple of years ago he was the one the police were after; now it's you."

Sparks's mouth gaped open, showing a lot of dirty teeth. "Tadeusz? Wasn't he –"

"Shut up, Sparks," said Cap. "Yeah, 'course I remember Tadeusz. I worked for him – a cheapskate, I always thought. But he's dead, Jim."

Sparks nodded his head vigorously. "In the lane," he said. "Behind the restaurant."

"Shut *up*, Sparks."

Coffee puddled on the floor. Cap went over to the kitchen area, washed his hands at the sink, dried them carefully on a towel. A fastidious guy. Tadeusz watched him carefully.

"Yeah, he's dead," I said. "But his ghost is still around. And I can see him now. He's on the back of the couch."

I pointed.

Sparks whirled around. "Where?"

Fear in his voice. Sparks was totally superstitious – like a kid, or a Viking. Once, during a storm he had confided in me that he feared the thunder giants.

"I see nothing," he whispered.

"He's sitting there," I said, "with his hands folded. Nodding at me now – hi, Tadeusz." I waved. "He's still dressed okay – got a suit on. But it's wrinkled. And of course there are bullet holes in it."

Sparks took a step back. "Bullets," he said.

"He's kidding, Sparks," said Cap. "Aren't you, Jim?"

"Nope."

I wasn't freaked seeing Tadeusz. I'd seen Morgan at the hospital. I knew that there were ghosts out there. Yes, it was odd to see a floating gray figure in Cap's living room. But Tadeusz was a reminder of what I was trying to do with my life, what I did *not* want to become. And he was on my side – he didn't want me to end up like him either. He was a friend, in a way that Cap and Sparks weren't.

Sparks wriggled, as if there was a beetle crawling up his back.

"Is he still there, Jim? What's he doing?"

"He's shaking his head."

"Is he angry at me?"

Sparks had a gristly knot of a nose, and it twitched now.

"Why would he be angry?"

"Because of what happened behind the restaurant. When Cap and I –"

"For the last time, *shut up!*" said Cap.

Sparks shivered. Scared, or maybe he could feel the chill coming off Tadeusz. I know I could.

"He's not angry," I said. "He's disappointed."

And puzzled, I could tell. His head was on one side and he was looking at Sparks and then at Cap.

"Oh! Oh! Oh!" Sparks jerked his head sideways. "I don't like this. Tell him to go away, Jim."

"There's no one here," said Cap. But Sparks was unconvinced.

"Tadeusz looks after me," I said. "Remember that. I don't want you walking up to me on the street and punching me. He'll be there. He'll put his hands on you, Sparks. His cold, cold hands. Do you want that?"

Sparks shook his head.

"He may even whisper in your ear," I said. "Just think – you'll feel his cold breath all down your neck."

"No!" Sparks was staring around wildly. "No! I don't want any ghost breathing on my neck!"

He ran to Cap's door, yanked it open, and disappeared into the hall, yelling something about ghosts and revenge. The door stayed open.

Now that I wasn't in danger, Tadeusz had no reason to be here. He rose off the back of the couch and floated across the room. He glared at Cap the whole time, even when his body was through the outside wall and I could only see his head. Something about Cap was really upsetting him.

Cap took off his cap, ran his hand over his head. "Would you go to Pineview and tell Raf to keep quiet, Jim? Would you do that for me?"

I'd never seen him bareheaded. He looked quite different with his clipped hair and a neat razor part. Almost pleasant.

I nodded. "I'll talk to Raf. What he does then is up to him. But get this straight, Cap – I'm not coming back."

"I don't want you back," said Cap. "Get out of here and close the door behind you. I want to change clothes."

I walked home with my head down. The dumpling clouds had spread to cover the sky, and it was starting to rain. I found a new box of Froot Loops, a carton of milk, and some maple cookies. I had a snack or maybe it was lunch, took my pill, and listened to the rain run off the eaves.

I couldn't keep my eyes open, so I went upstairs for a nap.

Music coming from my sister's room.

"Cassie!" I called.

No answer. I knocked on her door and called her name again.

"Go away!" she screamed. "Leave me alone!"

I wanted to talk to her, but I was just too beat. I went to bed and slept all the way through until late next morning.

Cassie was gone. I charged through another bowl of cereal, bought an apple I didn't really want, and went for a walk down Galley Avenue. Still no sign of Marcie or the car. Too bad because I could have told her about Tadeusz. She'd have been interested. I bet she could see ghosts too. It was something we had in common. She'd have laughed at Sparks running away.

And then it was one o'clock – visiting hours at the youth detention center. I hopped a 504 streetcar to the Dundas West Station, then a westbound train to Islington and a southbound bus to Pineview Terrace.

CHAPTER 27

Who picks street names? I could see no pine trees from Pineview Terrace. Junked cars, trash, and a couple of barbed-wire fences around the sooty brick detention center – that was the vista. The only green growing things were weeds.

I pushed my way through two sets of doors, signed in, waved at the security camera, held my hands up to be frisked.

Now there was something piney – a smell coming from the bucket in the corner of the room. They should have called it Pine-Sol Terrace.

So far I was the only visitor. I had the room to myself, me and the bucket and a bunch of little round tables. Quiet as snow.

I was feeling heavy inside. I didn't like Raf being in jail. And then there was the . . . I didn't know, the weird way it had all gone down. And when he came in, with a guard and a number on his green shirt and that smile that lit up his face, I felt even heavier.

"Hey, Jim! They told me I had a visitor, but they didn't say who."

Sparks hadn't recognized me without hair, but Raf did. I waved.

"Great to see you! I thought you were dead, man. I heard you got run over!"

The guard had his thumbs in his belt. A lip licker –
I didn't trust him.

Up close I saw that Raf had the remains of a black
eye and a bruise high up on his forehead.

"Yeah, I got run over," I said. "I was in hospital."

"I'm real glad you came."

I felt *sorry* rising inside me like an elevator. We sat at
one of the round tables, and I reached into my pocket.

"*Hey!*" The guard moved forward. "What do you
have there?"

I held up my hand. He relaxed. I gave my gift to
Rafal.

"Crispy Crunch, my favorite."

"I know."

While he ate, I told him what Cap had said about
not talking to the cops.

Raf frowned, like I was stupid. "They already offered
a deal," he said. "If I testify against Cap and Jerry, I go
free. The cops know all about the car-theft ring, they just
don't have any proof. Did you know Cap cleared more
than half a million dollars last year? That's how come he
can afford to hire my lawyer. But he doesn't have to worry
about me. I'm not talking to any cops."

Defiantly, he took another bite of chocolate.

I looked at his fading black eye.

"I'm sorry, Raf," I said.

"Sorry? For what?"

"For running away. There was that weird noise
coming from the backseat and I bailed. And when I saw

the cop car cruising down the alley, I didn't go back to warn you. I hopped a fence and kept running. Cap sent me today, but I was coming anyway. I had to say sorry."

The people you let down, Tadeusz had told me. I had let Raf down, all right. I didn't want to be a criminal anymore, but I had trouble looking at my old partner.

Raf swallowed his mouthful and did the strangest thing. He laughed.

"Sorry? You're sorry?"

"Yeah."

"Why are you sorry for not getting caught? Would you rather we were both here? Would that make you feel better?"

"It was such a weird noise," I said. "I couldn't –"

"I don't want anyone being sorry for me. I'm fine. Got a lawyer, don't I? Got movies to watch, dormitory gangs to fight with, counselors to lie to, and I never see my dad. Okay with me. It's not your fault the cops came, Jim. Somebody saw us go into the garage and called 911. You got out at the last possible moment. It was already too late for me."

"Really?"

"Yeah."

I flopped against the back of my chair. "Huh!" I said.

"That's more like it. Let's see that beautiful smile now."

Other visitors arrived. Moms, mostly. Some brothers and sisters. One little girl clutched a black-and-white kitten. There was a NO ANIMALS sign, but the kitten was so small the guard didn't notice it. He licked his lips and stared off into space.

Raf had his head turned sideways, staring at me out of the corner of his eye.

"So you had to say sorry, did you, Jim? You had to come out here to apologize? What is *with* you, man?"

Rafal was my best friend. We talked about sports and TV shows, and girls, and different kinds of potato chips, and would there be flying cars in the future. You know the kind of stuff. It was all here, all *real*. (Well, not the flying cars.) We talked about the life we knew.

I still liked him, but I couldn't tell him anything about my life now. I couldn't talk about seeing ghosts and memories, and trying not to be a piece of crap anymore. He wouldn't understand. He'd be . . . embarrassed for me. So I kept it simple, and told him about waking up in hospital, glad to be alive, and sorry for that night in the Lincoln. He finished the chocolate bar, licked his fingers and around his mouth, then opened the wrapper on the table and licked the inside of it.

"Okay, so you're sorry. Got it. Can we talk about something else?"

"Did you ever find out what the noise was?" I asked.

He shrugged. "It stopped by the time the cops got there. Bastards."

"Bastards," I agreed. But my heart wasn't really in it. I was glad I'd come to visit, glad Raf didn't hate me for walking around while he was in jail. But I was pretty sure he'd go back to boosting cars when he got out. We'd never be as close as we had been.

I thought of my past as a burning building. I had jumped, and hoped to land safely. But jumping is a one-way trip: you can't change your mind halfway down.

CHAPTER 28

A worn-out lady came into the visiting area pushing a bundle buggy. She picked a table away from ours and sat with a sigh. The kid she was visiting was a few years younger than Raf or me. He sat up straight in his chair. His eyes were all over the place. She was way too old to be his mom – grandma, maybe.

Raf noticed me staring. "That's Joel," he said in a low voice. "He's crazy."

Joel was biting the pads of skin at the top of his fingers. Grandma took a Twinkie out of her bundle buggy and offered it to him. He stared at it and went back to his fingers.

"He screams every night," said Raf. "We leave him alone. He's got, like, marks all over his back."

"What's he in for?"

"They say he tortured a baby girl – held her over a candle flame."

We were both quiet.

"What's wrong, Jim?"

"Nothing." I blinked. "Nothing. Did Joel give you the black eye?"

"Nah, that was Stevie. We were arguing about an old movie they had us watching. Ever seen *Driving Miss Daisy*?"

"No."

"Well, there's an old black guy who drives an old

white lady around, and that's pretty much the whole movie. Point is, the chauffeur was that guy who usually plays God or the president. He's got a great voice, talks real slow and careful. You know the guy I mean, Jim?"

"Sure. That guy. He was in *Seven* and a bunch of other stuff."

"Yeah. What's his name?"

"I can't remember. I know who you mean, though."

"Well, Stevie said it was the guy who plays Darth Vader. That voice, you know. 'Luke, I'm your father.' That guy. I told Stevie he was an idiot, and we got to fighting and he popped me. Stevie's had it in for me ever since he came. He wanted my bunk, and I wouldn't give it up."

"*Driving Miss Daisy*, eh?" I said. "Sounds lame."

"Shut up, it was pretty good."

I watched the boy Joel. He sat up straight as an iron bar. His back never touched the back of the chair.

Commotion across the room. The kitten was loose on the floor. The little girl and her mom were trying to catch it.

"Hey!" called the guard. "No animals."

The mom was on her hands and knees, trying to coax the kitten from under the table. Stupid thing leapt over her hands, raced past the girl and the guard, and made a beeline for Joel. He gave a sort of a convulsive twitch and grabbed it around the middle. It struggled, but he held on with both hands.

"Ho ho!" he said. "Ho ho ho!" He had a deep croaking voice for a little kid. All that screaming, I guess. The kitten mewed unhappily.

Raf was on his feet real fast. "Joel," he said.

The little girl went to get her pet back.

"Joel," said Raf. "Give the girl her kitten."

He's funny about animals. Last summer we were walking across the parking lot at the supermarket, and there was this dog locked in a car with the windows up. Raf grabbed a rock and busted one of the windows. Then he ran into the supermarket and stole a bottle of water. I told him he was crazy, but he just smiled, holding that dog under one arm and letting it lick the water a bit at a time. He's the sort of guy who can put out his hand and a bird will land on it.

Joel didn't want to let the kitten go. He held it close to his face and stared at it, the whites of his eyes showing all around the dark bit in the middle. He wanted to hurt the kitten. Just looking at him, you knew that's what he was thinking.

My heart was racing. I hate cats. I hate the sound they make. I felt like I was about to choke.

Joel's grandma hadn't moved. Stunned, maybe. Or just plain tired of Joel. Raf marched over and took the kitten. Joel looked around like he didn't know where he was.

Raf stroked the kitten, calming it. Then he gave it to the little girl.

"No animals," said the guard.

"Sorry," called the girl's mom. "But our car window broke. If I leave her in the car she'll run away. And I can't put her in the trunk."

The trunk.

"You can't have the cat in here," said the guard. "It's not allowed."

The trunk.

The little girl carried her kitten outside, while her mom said good-bye to a kid with a swastika tattooed on his neck. Classy.

The guard led Joel away.

"Raf," I said.

"You okay, Jim?"

"No. Listen, Raf. The weird noise in the back of the Lincoln. What if it was an animal? That kitten sounded familiar."

"There was no animal in the backseat," he said.

"What about in the trunk?"

He stared past me, trying to remember. "Maybe," he said. "Maybe the noise came from the trunk. Damn!"

Joel's grandma walked slowly to the outside door, dragging her bundle buggy as if her whole sorry life was in it.

"What if it *was* an animal?" said Raf. He smacked his fist into his palm. "A cat or a dog. Damn. I hate that! You can't keep animals in the trunk of a car. They'll die!"

I was thinking of Wolfgang and me, floating down toward Roncy in my second vision. *I know what you're scared of*, he told me. *I see you . . .*

Raf grabbed my arm. "Jim, you got to do something for me. Go back to the garage and check. Tonight, okay? I can't stand the idea of a trapped animal."

My face probably gave away what I thought. I didn't want to break into any cars. I sure didn't want to break into a car where they caught us last time. And I especially for sure did not want to break into a trunk with a cat in it.

I could feel sweat on my palms, just thinking about it.

"It's been ages," I said. "If there was an animal in the trunk, it's probably dead."

"Probably, but not for sure."

"Didn't the cops search the trunk?"

"Naw. They found me in the backseat with my tools and took me in right away."

"I dunno, Raf."

"What if the animal's still alive? Or there might be another one. Maybe the trunk is where he keeps them."

"Aw, Raf."

"Please, Jim."

Raf had never asked me for anything before. Never.

I thought about being a piece of crap. What made you a piece of crap, anyway? Breaking the law, or letting down a friend?

I wiped my palms on my pants. Nodded my head.

"'Kay," I said.

"Off Pearson, the first alley past Roncesvalles. Remember, it's a big white Lincoln. The garage has no door."

"I remember. I'll do it."

"Tonight, Jim."

"I said I'll do it."

"'Kay. Thanks."

He punched me on the shoulder. I punched him back. And left.

On the way out I heard the guard talking on his cell phone. "Not now, Zelda baby," he said. "I'm at work. I can't talk at work."

CHAPTER 29

When I got home, I finished off the maple cookies and went upstairs for a nap, feeling kind of, well, horny, but I fell asleep before I could do anything about it. My dream wasn't sexy at all. It began as a memory. I was in the alley between Galley Avenue and Pearson, ducking into the garage to help Raf fiddle the car door. A heavy door, because this was a Lincoln Town Car, longest thing on the road. "Trunk big enough for an elephant," said Raf. He was under the steering column while I held the flashlight for him. We heard the noise behind us. And now the scene started to spin like a paint wheel, memory bleeding into nightmare. I forced my head around enough to see out of the corner of my eye. In the backseat was an enormous gray cat. It licked its paw, over and over, tongue the size of a hand towel. It mewed again, loud enough to make the car vibrate. Then the beast leaped over the seat and landed on me, knocking me sideways. I sprawled along the roomy bench seat of the Lincoln with the cat sitting on my chest, heavy, hairy, and *soaking wet*. My shirt was drenched. The cat shook itself, and a wave of water rolled toward me. I woke up to screaming.

Late afternoon. My room faced west, and the sun was streaming in.

Cassie screamed again. She stood in my doorway, pointing down at the floor. "It's crawling under your bed!" she cried.

"What is?"

"The thing!"

She sighed. "But you can't see it. 'Course you can't – even though it was sitting on *your* chest. A horrible thing, whispering in your ear. Oh! It's still there! Sucking its thumb like an evil child!"

I peered over the edge of the bed, and saw –

"Oh, yeah," I said. "Hi, Wolfgang."

He took his thumb out of his mouth, waved. There'd been something familiar about the cat in my dream. The way it licked its paw. The wetness.

Wolfgang.

And now I understood. "So *this* is how you visit," I said to him. "You show up when I am asleep. Right?"

Grave Walkers were part of our nightmares. They were tied to Earth by fear, and nightmares are pure fear. That's how Wolfgang knew I hated cats.

He nodded. Beads of sweat on his face.

"*You* . . ." Cassie stared from me to Wolfgang and back again. "You see it too, Jim? Oh, God, you *do*!"

Wolfgang was floating away. I watched him drift through my window, disappearing in the sun's glare.

"It's true!" whispered Cassie. "I knew it! I knew it!"

"What?"

She had her hand to her mouth, backing out of my room.

"You're dead! You died in the accident."

She turned and ran. I followed her.

"Wait!" I cried.

"You've been dead all along!"

She tried to slam her room door but I got my hand in the way, and held it open.

"Go away! Leave me alone!"

"Come on, Cass. We have to talk."

"No!"

I used my shoulder on the door. Terror gave her strength, but I outweighed her by fifty pounds. I pushed my way into her room. She retreated to the far wall and stood shivering against the bubbled blue-and-white wallpaper she had hung up herself. She was wearing a tight top that showed sweat stains. Her eyes were wide and staring.

I stayed by the door. Didn't want to scare her even more.

"I'm not dead," I said calmly.

"Yes you are. You died in the hospital. Ma said so."

"No she didn't."

"She said you weren't yourself."

"Yeah, but I wasn't dead. Come on, Cass, I'm not a ghost. I'm wearing different clothes."

"Ghosts can do that."

"I talk to Ma."

"Ma's crazy. Or drunk. Who knows what she sees."

She had a point there. I tried to think how to put it. How do you prove you're alive?

"If I was a ghost, I wouldn't need to push the door open, would I, Cass. I'd just walk through it."

She shook her head. Stubborn.

"You think I'm dead because I could see that Grave Walker in my bedroom just now. But you saw him too, Cass. And you're alive."

"You don't understand. I saw *you*, Jim," she said. "I saw you *dead*."

"Yeah, I know. A couple of years ago, in the living room. You looked in the corner and saw two shadowy guys. And one of them was me, in my dragon shirt. *Peek-a-boo*, you said. But I wasn't a ghost, Cass. I was in a coma, revisiting the past. I survived. I woke up in the hospital and came home. Yes, I am different. I can see ghosts. But I don't want to become one. They're all pieces of crap, you know. It was a ghost who told me this."

I took a deep breath. "And that's why I want to talk to you, sis."

I told her the whole thing: Tadeusz and his warning, the door in the sky, the crappy Jordan Arms, my past on the TV screens, the emergency ambulance ride and near-death, waking up in the hospital, and slowly realizing how different I was.

I told her about everything except Marcie. That was a private hope I didn't want to share.

Cassie listened hard, frowning in concentration. She kept shaking her head, but I know she believed me.

"I remember that Tadeusz guy," she said. "Louise's mom used to cut his hair. He'd give her a twenty-dollar tip every time. Huh. Huh. And now he's worried about you, turning out bad like him. So pathetic."

I didn't say anything.

"Why can't they leave us alone? Stay in their stupid hotel and drink their stupid ginger ale." She was staring out the window at the empty school yard next door. She turned suddenly. "What's with that, anyway? Who ever heard of ghosts eating or drinking?"

"I don't know," I said. "But these are the spirits who are still tied to Earth. Ghosts in stories have chains, don't they? Heavy, clanking chains that they have to drag around?"

She wasn't really listening. "We don't need them telling us to watch out. We sure don't need them in our nightmares."

"They're not here for us," I said. "Their own fear pulls them back. Or regret. Or anger."

"Anger."

She smiled. Not nicely. "How long has that Slayer – the pirate guy – been around?"

"Morgan? A long time."

"And was he going to kill you? Is that what Slayers do?"

"I don't know. Maybe. I saw him in the hospital when Chester died. I think Slayers are drawn to death, the way Grave Walkers are drawn to nightmares and Mourners are drawn to regret. That's why they tell you to watch out. They know something bad is coming."

"*Watch out.*" Her face tightened. "Yeah, I've heard *that* before."

"Tadeusz says that every ghost used to be a piece

of crap. I never found out Wolfgang's story, but I can guess. I bet he was a bully and a mean little kid, and he died terrified."

A shudder took hold of Cassie, and she shook herself like a dog coming out of the lake. When she turned to face me, there were tears in her eyes. "All my life, Jim," she said. "All my life. I didn't know if I was crazy, or what. No one else could see what I saw. And I've never told anyone – not even Louise."

"There, there," I said, sympathetic, like I was with the nurse, Bertha. I was going to give my sister a hug, but something held me back. Maybe the way she had her hands balled up into fists.

"Remember . . ." She took a deep breath. "Remember when that streetcar went off the tracks about five years ago?"

"Yeah, yeah. Down at the foot of Roncy. We talked about it in school."

A picture of the streetcar on its side, looking like a beached whale, had been all over the news. Couple of people had died.

"Well, I was *on* that streetcar before it crashed. Riding down Roncy, and suddenly there were all these ghosts, shaking their heads and yelling. Tapping people on the shoulder. *Watch out!* they said. *Watch out!* I was terrified. I got out at the next stop. Marion. Then I watched the streetcar roll down Roncy to King and turn the corner and flip over."

"You never said anything."

"What could I say?" she hissed. "Who would have believed me? I have dreams, Jim, where I'm in a stadium, and there's going to be a terrorist attack, and thousands and thousands of ghosts appear, shouting for everyone to watch out. All of us in the stadium are doomed, and I'm the only one who knows."

For a moment, I felt nothing but pity for her.

CHAPTER 30

Something I'd been meaning to ask. "Hey, Cassie, I know it was a long time ago, but do you remember seeing my ghost when you were really little? I was with a Mourner. Actually, it was Maq's mom, but you wouldn't know that. Anyway, do you remember? I guess you were four or five."

"No."

"I was a baby." I spoke steadily. "It was the time you pushed me down the stairs and wrecked my ankle."

She turned away. She remembered all right.

"I have always had this trick ankle, and it's your fault."

Did she say sorry? Not hardly. She turned back to glare at me. "Yeah, well, so what?"

"So what? So you hurt me."

The muscles and strings in her throat went up and down when she drank. She had no fat on her, Cassie. It was like staring at a drawing from a book of human anatomy.

"Uh-huh," she said.

Pretty bleak. I didn't know what to say to her. Her anger was stronger than my conviction.

The sounds and smells of a July afternoon drifted into the room. Kids screaming on the playground. Insects buzzing against the screen. Diesel exhaust. A snatch of a song on a car radio. Laughter. Away in the distance, a siren. A sharp whiff of barbecue from the house next door.

It occurred to me that it was thanks to my trick ankle that I got run over in the first place. If it weren't for Cassie wrecking my ankle, I'd never have fallen. I'd still be a piece of crap, like Tadeusz. Funny how things work out sometimes.

She relaxed on the bed. Her hands weren't fists anymore. Her face softened slightly. "All right, maybe I was a rotten sister."

Was this an apology? I could forgive her, but she'd probably laugh at me. And I had been crappy to her too.

"But I did save your life once, Jim."

"What?"

"When the cat got in."

You ever been on the Drop-Zone ride at the amusement park? You know that feeling when the chair drops and your stomach stays up? That's how I felt then.

"What cat?"

"I don't know. Some ginger cat from the neighborhood. You were really small, just a baby. And this cat snuck in through the kitchen window. I remember petting it for a while and then forgetting about it. I went upstairs when I heard it mewing and there it was in your crib, sitting on you. I guess you don't remember."

"On me?"

"Yeah, right on your chest. It had its head right next to yours, mewing at you, and sort of batting at you with its paw. Hey, what's wrong?"

"Nothing."

"You look like you're going to be sick."

"I'm okay. Did the cat . . ." I took a breath and tried again. "Did it scratch me?"

"Nah. I think it just wanted to play. I took it outside. All right, maybe I didn't actually save your life, but you did look pretty unhappy there in your crib. Crying, you know. You didn't cry much."

I sat carefully on the edge of Cassie's bed. Stared in front of me. Her dresser was tall and painted white. It had four drawers. The top one was partly open. She had a picture from a magazine taped to the wall over the dresser. A family, it looked like. A mom, dad, two kids. The dad wore glasses. The little girl had a bow in her hair. They were all sitting around the dining room table, laughing.

A cat in my crib. *A cat in my crib.*

"Son of a bitch," I said.

We went downstairs for a snack. Not much in the cupboard. Ma had a lot of Old Mother Hubbard in her. I made a Froot Loop sandwich, with jam to hold it together. When I offered to make one for Cassie, she frowned.

"You really are different, Jim. Ever since you came back from hospital. You're like Scrooge in that movie."

"Who?"

"*You* know. The mean old guy in London. The ghost of Christmas past shows him he's been bad, and he changes his life. Gonzo was in it, and Kermit."

"Oh, sure. And Tiny Tom," I said.

"Tiny Tim."

"Whatever."

Come to think of it, I was kind of Scrooge-y. Stealing fruit and cars, and beating people up was like forcing poor Kermit to work on Christmas. Denise, Wolfgang, and Morgan were the ghosts. Now I'd woken up, and I was different. Like Scrooge. Hah. Not bad. At the end of the movie he's happy.

She poured herself a glass of water. I asked for one too. She poured it and then slammed it on the table. "Don't expect *me* to turn nice," she said.

My sis. I was glad I'd talked to her. It was a relief to share this huge thing, this knowledge, with someone who understood. For almost the first time in our lives, we connected. Freak-os together. I told her about trying to pay back Mr. K. She didn't think it was funny.

"It's what Scrooge would do," I said.

"I hate Tiny Tim," she said.

CHAPTER 31

Cassie went out for dinner with Louise. I stayed at home and worried about what I might find when I broke into the Lincoln's trunk later that night. A cat, say. How about that for a revelation? Cassie's cat story, I mean. Talk about your anti-climax. I walked around the empty house, feeling anxious, giggly, embarrassed, then anxious again. I ate handfuls of Froot Loops, drank milk from the container. I made my bed. I kept having to pee.

Now I was flipping through the TV with the sound down. The clock on The Weather Channel was exactly one minute behind my digital watch. *The Simpsons* episode was the one where Marge becomes a cop. I turned up the sound to hear Chief Wiggum say he wouldn't give the psycho a gun until he knew his name. I laughed and kept flipping. It was getting dark.

Ma came home and fell onto the couch beside me. "Jim Jim Jimmie," she said, sort of singing. "How's my poor boy?" Her makeup was smudged, and she smelled of cigarettes and liquor.

"Fine," I said.

"I haven't seen you in a while, sleepyhead. I'm glad you're looking better. Your hair is coming in nicely."

The Weather Channel had caught up to my watch. They now both said 9:18.

The weather guy was talking about forest fires out west. They were a big story. We watched this one tree burn for thirty seconds. I really got into it. At first it seemed like a sexy dance between the tree and the fire, the flames climbing slowly up the trunk, saying, Come on, honey, while the tree shivered like, No thank you. The fire spread along the branches like, You know you want to! But the tree shook back and forth like, No! No! Please no! It wasn't a dance anymore. There was an explosion, and the fire was suddenly huge and happy, and all over the tree. And the tree was crying.

The segment ended. I flipped up and down the TV, finding nothing but commercials.

I wanted to ask Ma about the cat getting in, because the whole thing was still freaking me out. But she hadn't been there. Instead, I asked her what she remembered about my dad.

She was falling asleep. "Your father?" she muttered. "That prick. 'Course I remember him."

"You do?"

"What do you think I am, some kind of slut? His name was Walter. He had red hair and eyes like winter."

"Did he get sick when I was born?"

"Walter? No. Cassie got sick. They thought she was going to die. Walter was arrested for credit card fraud and skipped bail."

"Oh."

I watched an old music video where flakes of soot fell on dying children. I thought about Cassie getting very sick. Did she get to the Jordan Arms? That'd explain how she could see ghosts.

When I flipped back to *The Simpsons* Marge had quit the police force and Moe was playing poker with the counterfeit jeans guy.

"Do you think he loved us?" I said.

Ma snuggled against me. She was falling asleep. "Who?"

"Skip it."

She yawned wide enough to swallow a tennis ball. Her head fell back against the cushions and she started to snore.

I went upstairs and opened the spiral notebook.

Dr. Driver said to put down my memories, and that's what I've been doing. I'm surprised at how regular I've been. It helped that I've spent so much time in my room. I mean, there I'd be, yawning, and there was the notebook lying open on my bed or on the orange crate I use as my bedside table. I'd write a page or two and then fall asleep, and when I'd wake up there it'd be, ready to hand. There are lots of blank pages left in the book, but I don't know how much more I have to say. I've written down everything that happened from the day I got run over until now. When is a story finished? I dunno. When the notebook's full?

I keep my tools hidden under the floorboards of my closet. I take them out and put them on the table. Flashlight, sharpened screwdriver, plastic shim, and a hook made from a half a coat hanger. Raf uses a set of blank car keys, but it takes just as long to find the right one as it does to use the shim and hook. I put on a black long-sleeved shirt and check the time. 10:46. Still way too early to go.

CHAPTER 32

One final entry in this book. A lot *almost* happened in the last hour. It's still too early to go, so I'll take a few minutes, sitting here at the bottom of my bed next to Louise's bare toes.

What did happen is that Cassie came home with her friend. They were flushed and couldn't stop giggling. "Hi, little brother," said Louise.

"No, no," said Cassie. "He's my little brother, not yours."

They blinked at me. We were in the hall upstairs. I could hear Ma snoring in the living room.

Louise gave me the down-up look. "He's not *that* little."

Neither was she. She was wearing a T-shirt with a picture of SpongeBob on it. His goggle eyes were a lot closer to me than his feet, if you know what I mean. When she shook her head back and forth, it looked like SpongeBob was caught in a typhoon. Her hair fell in front of her face and stayed there.

"Jim's almost as cute as that one waiter," said Louise.

"Uh-huh," said Cassie.

"I still don't know why you dragged us away. He liked us. They both did. I wish we could have stayed."

"Jim'll understand."

Louise was going to say something but stopped dead. "Who's Jim'll?"

"Jim'll?" said Cassie.

"You said Jim'll understand," said Louise.

They giggled and said *Jim'll* a couple of times.

"Well, he *will* understand," said my sister. "Won't you, Jim'll?"

She'd seen a Mourner. That's why she knew I'd understand. "We were drinking chocolatinis, and I heard someone say, '*Watch out*.'" Cassie nodded meaningfully at me. "I turned around and there he was, floating behind me."

"I didn't hear anything," said Louise. "Or see anything. The waiters were smiling at us. I wanted to stay."

She put her hand on the wall to support herself. Meanwhile, Cassie's meaningful look had turned to one of concern. She blinked at me.

"I . . . bathroom," she said, stumbling past me. I wondered how many chocolatinis she'd had.

Louise lurched against me. She put her arms around my neck. "Hey there, Jim'll," she said. "You may not be as cute as the waiter, but you are pretty cute. And you're here."

She rubbed SpongeBob against me.

I thought about Ma downstairs and Cassie in the washroom.

I thought about Marcie. I saw her smile and her teddy-bear dressing gown. I heard her saying she liked me. Felt her lips on my cheek.

"Put your arms around me," said Louise. She stood on her tiptoes to bring her mouth up against mine and kissed me. I mean, really kissed me.

I stopped thinking about Marcie.

I remembered the forest fire creeping up the tree. I felt like that myself. It was a long way around Louise. I squeezed her tight. She moved her mouth on mine and kissed me again. Yikes. Her tongue seemed to reach into my stomach. You could say that I burst into flame. We kissed some more.

Louise took one hand away from my neck and ran it down my chest and stomach, down past the bottom of my black shirt to the front of my jeans.

Ta-da! said my dick.

She grabbed one of my empty belt loops and walked backward, dragging me after her.

"This is your room, right, Jim'll?"

Clothes in a corner, Ferrari poster on the wall, newly made bed with *Star Wars* sheets, a table made from an orange crate holding some tools and a nearly full spiral notebook. My room.

I stood in the doorway. Louise put her hands over her head and tried to twirl like a ballet dancer. She wobbled and fell backward onto the bed. She was wearing slip-on sandals, I noticed, and one of them had fallen off. Her toenails were painted bright red.

Unmistakable noises were coming through the bathroom door. I tried to ignore them and focus on Louise. She was lying on her back now, breathing deeply. Looked like the tide was coming in.

Ta-da! said my dick.

My sister finished throwing up. I heard the toilet flush, but she didn't come out. Louise's eyes were closed. These girls could not drink.

I heard snoring from behind the bathroom door. I looked in. Cassie was asleep, curled around the toilet bowl. Back in my room, Louise had rolled onto her side, pillowing her head in her hands. Her eyes were closed; her expression innocent, childlike.

I got a picture of myself, a horny teen with a drunken woman in his bed and she's fast asleep. I threw back my head and laughed. *Ta-da!* said my dick. But that only made me laugh some more. I got my spiral note-book out and sat down gingerly next to Louise.

I'm done writing now. It's midnight. I'm about to grab my tools and leave.

I'm not looking forward to the next bit.

CHAPTER 33

I hurry down Roncesvalles past Galley to Pearson Avenue. I hear music and TV noise coming from the apartments over the stores, and pigeons cooing from rooftops. The air is warm and greasy.

My tools weigh in my pocket. Flashlight doesn't mean anything, and the hook's just a piece of bent wire, but the sharpened screwdriver's a weapon, and the bendy shim screams, *Car thief!* You use it to pry the window away from the doorframe so you can reach the hook in and open the door. If the cops search me, they're going to be suspicious.

I don't want to be here. Ol' Scrooge wouldn't be doing this. But Scrooge didn't have a promise to keep. I won't let Raf down.

I get a bit of a shiver, turning onto Pearson. Last time I walked this way I was with Raf. That was only a few weeks ago, but I feel a million years older.

The alley off Pearson is a long shared driveway with garages on both sides. It's lit by a couple of streetlights on wooden poles. One of them is flickering, making the shadows dance. Walking down the alley under the flickering light, I kind of lose myself. Doesn't last long but the feeling is strong, like a dream vision. It seems for a moment that the garages are moving and I'm the one staying still – like I'm on a station platform watching two freight trains flash by. They're on their way to the future, and I'm stuck here forever in this present.

The white Lincoln is in a garage with no door, facing out, just like I remember. There's a NO PARKING sign across the alley, next to a BEWARE OF DOG sign. Someone has been by with a can of spray paint, so the first sign looks like it reads, NO BARKING. Ha ha.

The hood of the big car gleams in the harsh light. No sound coming from the yard, no lights in the house. I slip into the garage.

I check the car door because it might be open. It isn't. I pull out my tools, and in less time than it takes me to write this, I slide in the shim and hook the opener. You sometimes have to fish around, but I get it right away.

I'm totally concentrating on the job because you don't want to jerk too hard and jam something. Out of the corner of my ear, I hear footsteps. I freeze. Two sets of footsteps in the alley and a murmur of voices growing louder. I'm up to the elbow in illegal tools and car door guts, and two guys are coming toward me.

I've got about four seconds to decide what to do. Plenty of time. The hook is in my right hand. I pull straight up and not too hard, and the door unlocks. Good to know I haven't lost my touch. I drop my tools into my pocket and slide around to the back of the garage, crouching low, peering around the rear bumper.

Two guys go past, dressed in black and white – waiters. "I still don't believe the tits on that girl," says one of them.

"I tell you, she was underage," says the other. "So was her skinny friend. We shouldn't even have served them the chocolatinis."

"I wonder why they took off like that?"

"I don't know. It was a waste of Blue Nitro."

Their footsteps fade.

Now that my ear is pressed against the trunk, I can hear noises coming from inside. Something is moving around in there. I slide into the front seat, pop the trunk catch, and the alarm goes off.

News flash: alarms don't do much good. One night Raf and I set off a bunch of them and hung around, timing reactions. The cops never showed. Not once. It took at least ten minutes for the owner to come – which is about nine minutes longer than it would take us to boost the car. One grumpy neighbor showed up way before the owner – and got so mad he kicked a dent in the front bumper. Raf and I killed ourselves laughing. I bet if we told him we were going to steal the car, he'd have held our coats.

So when I hear the alarm on the Lincoln, I'm not worried about being caught. I'm thinking, Who puts an alarm on the *trunk*?

I'm out of the front seat, careful. The trunk light is on, throwing shadows around the back of the garage. I peer round the trunk door. Yes, I am worried there might be a cat in there. Old fears die hard.

What I see is a car blanket, and the top of a head of hair. There's a kid in the trunk. A big kid, not a baby. Good thing the Lincoln has all that space.

The alarm is hooked up to the car horn. *Honk honk honk honk!* (Sounds like a boring goose telling you about its day: *So we were, like, flying along, me and my buddies, and, like, we always fly in this V formation, so there was me, and my buddy Jake ahead of me, and my buddy Ted behind me, and sometimes there was land below us, and sometimes there was water below us, and we, like, kept flying along. Honk honk honk!*)

"Hey," I say over the noise of the alarm.

The kid sits up, a scrawny, pale, pathetic boy with mousy hair and long eyelashes and a striped pajama top.

"Lloyd?" I say.

He blinks, focusing his eyes. "Jim!" he cries.

My first thought is that he's been kidnapped. Someone is taking children and hiding them in the trunk of his car. Lloyd is his latest victim. There was a case like this, last year. The cops went house to house, and the local TV gave hourly updates.

"Don't hurt me," he says.

Is there anyone in my life I treated worse than Lloyd? I don't think so. It's not right that he's here, but it's right that I am here to help him.

"I won't hurt you, Lloyd." I smile at him for maybe the first time ever. "I'm going to help you out of here. Come on, let's go."

He shakes his head no. I can't hear what he's saying over the noise of the alarm.

I bend closer. "What?"

"I'm supposed to sleep here tonight," he says.

I don't understand. "This is a car. You are in the trunk of a car."

"It's punishment."

"No one sleeps in the trunk of a car. You're confused. Come on."

Lloyd shrinks away. I reach forward to grab a pajama-covered leg. It feels like a stick under my hands. There are neat round holes in the floor of the trunk. I'm shocked when I realize that they are breathing holes. The kidnapper drilled them so that his victims wouldn't suffocate.

That's a yuck, actually – shocked. You'll see why in a minute.

Honk honk honk honk!

I brace myself against the rear bumper, pulling hard. Lloyd struggles. He doesn't want to go with me. It's awful, but kind of funny too. A reformed bully tries to rescue his old victim, and the victim doesn't want any part of it.

Suddenly he goes rigid with terror. Not because of me. He's never been this scared of me, not even when I was punching him or peeing on his coat. I drop his legs and turn. A rickety wooden door swings open at the back of the garage. Someone's inside. The alarm's been honking for less than a minute, but Lloyd's kidnapper is not your regular householder. Of course he's going to come quickly.

"*Watch out!*" yells a familiar voice from over my head.

"Dad!" yells Lloyd.

There's a fizzing sound, and my world stops.

CHAPTER 34

I'm on the floor of the garage, and my right shoulder is on fire. I feel like I've been stomped by a rhinoceros. The air smells like after-the-lightning. My right side is numb.

The car alarm shuts off. I can hear the blood pounding in my ears.

A man in a dark tracksuit stands next to me. Looks like an old ninja. He's holding something in his hand. A flashlight or something. His voice is soft and sweet as cotton candy.

"Sorry, Dad," says Lloyd. His voice seems to come from far away.

"Sorry doesn't mow the lawn, son," says the man in the tracksuit. "You know that."

My brain is like an engine with a faulty ignition. It's turning over but not catching. What happened? What happened?

A shadowy figure floats near my head.

"Hi, uh, Raoul."

I don't know if I actually say the words, but I think them. Raoul is Marcie's Mourner. The bearded guy with the whiny voice. It takes me a second to remember his name. He waves at me.

"Maybe next time you could give me a bit more warning," I say.

He shrugs like, I did my best.

I struggle to sit up. My right arm shakes uncontrollably. The old ninja squats next to me. His hair is wispy, and his mouth is puckered up like he's about to kiss a baby on election day. "You're trespassing, puke," he says. "That's the second time this month you pukes have broken into my car. I'm going to teach you to respect what is mine."

He holds out the flashlight, only it's not a flashlight. Instead of a light, there are two little pointy things on the end, and a small spark between them. The spark makes a buzzing sound.

"This is a stun gun. When these terminals touch your skin, you'll feel seventy thousand volts running through you. Won't kill you, but it will put you down, disgusting puke that you are. What's your name?"

He sounds polite, like he's telling an old lady the way to the post office.

My name. I've forgotten my name. If he gives me a second . . .

But he doesn't. He reaches out, and the spark hits me like a hammer. I'm back on the floor of the garage, screaming, before I know it.

"I asked you a question, puke. What's your name?"

See what I mean about being shocked? Not a yuck at all, really. My head is aching. My mouth tastes funny. There's something wrong with my eyes, because there are lines of bright light everywhere I look. It's like I'm peering out at the world through the bars of a cage.

I can't help thinking back to the times at school, when I'd tease Lloyd by rubbing my socks on the carpet and giving him shocks. He'd pee his pants and start to cry. And I'd laugh.

My turn now.

"His name is Jim," says Lloyd.

"You *know* this puke?" Standing up, turning toward the trunk. "You know his name?"

The gentle voice makes me want to throw up.

"Jim goes to my school."

"Oh, Lloyd."

"What's wrong, Dad?"

"Why are you answering your friend's questions for him?"

"Trying to save you time, Dad. And he's not my friend."

"I think he is, Lloyd. You know his name. You answer his questions. I think this puke is your friend."

"No!"

Feeling and strength return to my arms. My brain is running again. I know that I have to get away from this wacko. I'm on my back near the trunk of the car. I push with my palms and heels, sliding along the cement floor. I do it again. Push by push, I slide up the side of the car away from Lloyd's dad. He doesn't notice me – too busy threatening his son.

"Do you like sleeping in the trunk?"

"No, Dad."

"Want to go back to your own bed?"

Lloyd says something I can't hear.

"Sorry doesn't buy groceries, son."

Lloyd makes that noise again – the whimper that sounds like a cat mewing. Still creeps me out.

What to do? I can't run. Can't hide. Can't fight. I need a place to rest. I'm under the driver-side door, and I remember that it's unlocked. I raise myself onto one elbow and reach for the door handle. The door opens, and the dome light comes on. Oops. Forgot about that. Quickly I roll into a kneeling position and begin to pull myself into the car.

The trunk shuts with a solid *thunk*. Lloyd's dad can see what is going on now, his view no longer blocked by the raised trunk.

"Hey!" he cries.

"*Watch out!*"

CHAPTER 35

Raoul's voice, of course. He's sitting in the passenger seat of the car. I glare at him as I try to lever my body inside.

"You *think*?" I say. "You think I might be in danger here?"

He holds out both palms like, I'm only doing my job.

"*Watch out!*" I mimic him. "Really helpful, Raoul. How about stopping the bad guy, huh?"

Raoul shrugs like, I wish I could, but I can't.

Lloyd's dad scrabbles around the car. I slam and lock the door just in time. He pounds on the glass. I'm panting from the exertion. I feel light-headed. The bars of light are dancing in front of my eyes.

"Get out of my car, you puke!" he shouts.

I give him the finger. Raoul does too. His beard moves. Raoul is actually smiling – for maybe the first time since his girlfriend fell off the roller coaster.

Lloyd's dad bites his lip so hard that blood comes out. Nice guy. Nice scary guy. I'm safe for now, but not for long. Really, I'm not much better off than Lloyd. Maybe I should help him along with myself.

Help Lloyd. The idea swims into my brain like a sick fish in a pool of sludgy water. Help Lloyd. The idea of running away again – leaving Lloyd as I left Raf – is beyond awful. I can't let Lloyd spend any more of his life with this guy. I just can't.

Help Lloyd. But how?

His dad runs around the back of the car. I crane my head and see his silhouette in the open doorway at the back of the garage. He disappears.

"Appreciate the company, Raoul," I say. "But I wish you'd *do* something."

He pats me on the shoulder. I can't feel it.

My head is full up with headache, like a sink full of water. Bands of light are zigzagging in front of my eyes. I remember Dr. Driver said flashing lights were serious. Go to the hospital, she said.

Yeah, sure. But first I have to help Lloyd. My life has come down to that one thing. Help Lloyd. But how? Scrooge had it easy – all he had to do was buy Kermit a turkey. I have to slay Grendel here.

An idea works its way past my headache into my mind. Simple, effective, and well within my power. Illegal, but so what. I duck under the steering column of the big Lincoln and empty the tools out of my pocket. Lloyd's dad is calling the cops or getting his car keys. Either way I've got about a minute. But a minute's all it takes. Flashlight in my teeth, I isolate the wires I need, strip the insulation and twist them together, and feel the familiar jolt of electricity running through my hand as the engine catches.

I have to smile, despite my headache. Here I am trying to save Lloyd by stealing his car and running away with him. How reformed am I?

Of course, I don't know how my plan will work out in the long run. I don't know where Lloyd and I will be next week, or even tomorrow morning. I don't know what we'll do for food, or money, or anything. But Lloyd will be at least one tankful of gas away from here. And anywhere – anywhere on this planet – is better than here. I know I'm doing the right thing. It's a strange comfort.

I shift into Drive.

"Watch out!" calls Raoul. Big eyes. Worried expression.

"*Now?*" I say. "Why should I watch out now? We're safe in the car. What can happen *now*, Raoul?"

I don't get it. I take my foot off the brake and the big car moves majestically out of the garage. For about a second, the trip is going well.

CHAPTER 36

Then there's a sickening crash, and my side of the windshield goes all spiderwebby as the glass cracks and splinters. I put on the brakes. Another crash bends the windshield in toward me. I don't know what to do. I can't drive blind. A third crash, and most of my side of the windshield disappears in a rain of glass bits. I can see. Not that I like what I'm looking at. Lloyd's dad is kneeling on the hood of the Lincoln in his tracksuit, holding a piece of pipe like a baseball bat. He must have run around the garage and grabbed the heaviest thing he could find.

I hit the accelerator and spin the steering wheel. The car jerks forward and to the left. Lloyd's dad slides across the hood. I stomp on the brakes, which should send him flying off the side of the car, but he manages to hang on to the far doorpost as the car skids to a stop.

It's weird to drive with a huge hole in your windshield. Like swimming with your mouth open.

Lloyd's dad snarls at me, his teeth flashing white under the flickering streetlight. He lets go of the doorpost to reach for me. I straighten the wheel and put the car in reverse. This move catches him by surprise. He slides away from me, clutches at a windshield wiper, breaks it, and flings himself forward to land spread-eagled on the hood. One hand snakes toward me, grabbing first the dash and then the steering wheel. The other hand follows.

Yes, that's right. Lloyd's dad and I are holding the steering wheel from opposite sides. I'm sitting in the driver's seat. He's lying facedown on the hood.

"Don't say it!" I tell Raoul, who is still beside me. "I know."

If the wheel's a clockface, my hands are at nine and three o'clock. Lloyd's dad's are inside mine, at about eleven and one. His fingernails are rimmed with dark blood. His knuckles are white with the strain of holding on. We reverse down the alley. I try to keep one eye over my shoulder, to steer, and the other on Lloyd's dad. The speedometer creeps up.

If I stop, he'll end up in my lap.

He wrenches the wheel to my left. The car veers drunkenly. I straighten us out. He does it again. There's a hydro pole in the mirror. It looks real close, and the mirror says, OBJECTS ARE CLOSER THAN THEY APPEAR. We miss the pole by a finger. I straighten us out again.

I have no plan. All I'm doing is reacting. I'm aware of Lloyd in the trunk. I don't want to smash into something and hurt him. I'm aware of my headache, sloshing around inside me.

We're angled toward a garage with a yellow door. I yank the wheel around. Too far! I pull to straighten us out, but Lloyd's dad is pulling *in the same direction I am*. Instinctively, I slam on the brakes, and we skid into a half-donut – what Raf calls a *croissant*. That's when the car ends up turned around so that it's facing away from where you were going. It's a stunt turn. I've pulled a few of them, fooling around in parking lots. This is my first one in reverse. I don't know how I manage it in the narrow alley.

Lloyd's dad is lying sideways across the hood, hanging on to the wheel with only one hand. His feet are dangling over the passenger side of the car. This is my chance. If I speed forward and then jam on the brakes, he'll fly off like a stone from a slingshot. I shift into Drive. The big old engine roars. The way is straight. The speedo gets up to forty real fast. I have my foot on the brake pedal when Lloyd's dad brings his free hand around. In it is the stun gun. He must have had it in the pocket of his track pants.

Raoul and I cry out together. The horrible old man lunges through the windshield, his arm at full stretch. The blue spark touches my hand.

I see things in vivid depth and in slow motion. A wooden fence on my left. Lloyd's dad slipping sideways, his eyes wide and scared. Flashing lights in my mirror. I also see stuff I shouldn't see – stuff I can't be seeing. The pain bubble running up my arm, exploding in bright colors all over the inside of my skull. The hydraulic system transmitting force to the pistons and callipers on the disk brakes of the Lincoln. The muscles in my arms and shoulders working together to turn the steering wheel sharply to the left.

Now the action speeds up. The wooden fence buckles and folds, and we're bumping across a backyard with trees and bushes and a real fountain in the middle. Floodlights blind me and we crash. I close my eyes to turn off the world.

When I open them, Lloyd's dad is lying in the wrecked fountain with his neck at a funny angle. I am slumped low in the seat, staring into the side mirror at a face that looks like mine. I press the trunk release button with my good hand. And close my eyes again. When I open them this time, Morgan the Slayer stands in front of the car, grinning in at me through the hole in the windshield. His filed teeth glisten in the bluish spotlights. Even at this distance I can feel the heat coming off him.

Oh crap, I think.

He is not here for me, though. He strides over to the fountain and picks up Lloyd's dad by the scruff of the neck. He shakes him hard, twice, the way a dog kills a rat. Tucks him under his arm. And leaps into the air.

All right.

I stagger out of the Lincoln. Emergency vehicles choke the laneway. Lights flash, walkie-talkies echo. There are uniforms all over the lawn. One of them is helping Lloyd out of the trunk. I hope he's okay. Two or three more check the body in the fountain. Two women stand on the back porch, hands to their faces, horrified. Mother and daughter, maybe. Look like they live here. A black-and-white dog races around, wagging its tail. The daughter calls the dog to her. Come, Scipio, she says.

The air smells wonderful. Dew-wet grass. Some kind of sweet flower. I take a deep breath and feel myself relaxing. I'm tired and I have a headache, but the bands in front of my eyes are gone. I feel – this sounds bizarre – pretty good.

A loud voice tells me to step away from the car, and I do. And then to raise my hands in the air, and I try to. I get one up, but the other arm won't move from my side.

And then we all go to the police station.

CHAPTER 37

Not right away. First we hang around the back-yard while the cops make phone calls and wait for orders. Then we go to the hospital, where a doctor checks out the burn marks on my bad arm. He asks if it hurts and I say yes. He asks why I'm smiling and I shrug. He writes something on a clipboard and goes next door to check on Lloyd, who is okay. Ten minutes later I'm in the back of a police car, on my way to 11 Division.

The police want statements from all of us. There's a dead man and property damage and they want to know who to blame. They start with me.

I tell my story to a sergeant whose skin hangs on her face in folds, like drapes or something. She asks questions in a slow, flat monotone. What was I doing in the Snelgrove garage so late at night? Where did I get the carjacking tools? Why did Mr. Snelgrove attack me? Why am I so happy?

I tell her the truth. Not the whole truth, but a lot of it. I was walking, heard a noise, went to check on it, got attacked, tried to escape by driving away, lost control of the car and crashed. I may have touched the tools, I say, but the car was running when I got into it.

All right, that part is a lie.

She doesn't believe me, but what she can do? I have never been arrested. She can't prove anything except joyriding.

"Why are you smiling, Jim?" she asks again.

"Me? Smiling?"

She pushes skin away from her eyes so she can glare at me.

"You're doing it right now. You like to laugh at cops, Jim? This is no laughing matter, you know. You're in real trouble. You've broken the law and a man is dead. What is so funny?"

"I don't know," I say. "I guess I'm just a happy person."

She sends me back to the tiny waiting room and its plastic chairs. I sit beside a tiny woman with eyes that dart around and with a voice like rustling paper. Lloyd's mom. She's here because they wanted a grown-up present when they questioned Lloyd. (They called my house, even sent a car over, but no one answered the phone or the door.)

Lloyd sits on the other side of his mom. The two of them are holding hands. They look like Christmas morning. I can't imagine what it was like living in their house. Can't imagine it.

I've already said sorry. I don't know if he heard me. I try it again.

"Sorry for what?"

"For everything. You know. Everything. I'm . . . I'm a . . ."

"It's okay."

"*I* think you're a brave boy," says his mom.

"Thanks, Mrs. Snelgrove."

A door slams somewhere in the building and they jump, fear on their faces as clear as a bloodstain. They catch themselves, laugh, and settle back into their chairs again.

The sergeant with the drooping face skin comes into the waiting room, along with the mom and daughter from the wrecked backyard. I get up, and the daughter comes over to take my hand in both of hers. She smells of soap and sunshine.

"So, are they going to arrest you, Jim?" she asks.

"I don't know, Marcie. And I don't care."

She's the reason I'm smiling. I've been smiling pretty constantly ever since I recognized her on the back porch and realized that it was her fence I'd crashed through, her water feature I'd smashed. She recognized me too, and we sat on lawn chairs while we were waiting for the cops, and I told her Lloyd's story. In fact, I told her everything that had happened since Morgan dragged me away to make his grog. She cried and squeezed my hand. Her mom came over and said it was nice to see me again. Marcie wiped her eyes. The dog Scipio jumped up and licked my face.

There are statements for us to sign. A cop with a pot-belly and sniffles hands them out. The sergeant stands in the doorway, yawning and kneading her face.

ACKNOWLEDGMENTS

Some books seem to write themselves. Not this one. I have been tinkering with *Me & Death* for about five years. The trick was to balance humor and horror. Lengthy emails bounced back and forth among my publisher, my agent, and me, and revisions piled up like autumn leaves. Last year I faced a choice between a total rewrite and a nervous breakdown. And now that I am out of the hospital, I can honestly say that I have never felt better about the book.

Joking aside, I would like to express my heartfelt thanks to both Kathy Lowinger and Scott Treimel (forget what I said at the time) for their hours and hours and I say again *hours* of hard work on the story. Other people helped too: my son Sam, who drew the ghosts for me; my copy editor, Heather Sangster, who gave in gracefully now and then; and critical readers in Canada, the United States, and Ireland for their words of encouragement. Special thanks to all the people who sent in book covers for the website contest. Much appreciated. And finally, a sincere thank you to the Canada Council for help with this project.

One last point. Quite serious, this one. The idea of an afterlife book had been floating around in my mind for a while, but I didn't start to write *Me & Death* until I came across a story about a dad in Texas who was arrested for mistreating his five-year-old son. Without going into details, I'll say that Lloyd's dad in my story is drawn from him. Yeah, I know. Creepy, eh? I am no social reformer, believe me – just a guy who likes to connect with my readers, make them laugh and think. But whenever I felt like quitting the book, switching to a story about zombies or something, I would remember that poor kid and dial back in.

They don't want to let me go until they sort out what to do about Lloyd's dad's death. Apparently I could be charged with vehicular manslaughter, which sounds bad. When she hears this, Mrs. Snelgrove snorts. A loud noise for a tiny woman. "They should give you a medal," she says. And everyone is real quiet.

Marcie's mom volunteers to take me home and make sure I get back to the police station the next morning.

"You sure you want that responsibility, ma'am?" says the sergeant.

"Yes."

"She's a swing-shift manager," says Marcie. "She's used to responsibility."

Lloyd and I shake hands on the way out. I'm sure I'll do stupid things again, maybe even mean things, but not to him.

The sniffling cop sneezes three times into a tissue.

"Bless you," says Lloyd.

So I ride home in the same blue Pontiac that ran over me. Marcie falls asleep in the front seat, next to her mom. I look out the window at the stars, and the streetlights, and the oncoming headlights, and wonder about everything.